Have you heard the one about...

"I ain't letting any strange man in," the woman snapped. "This scattergun is getting heavy, and if you don't light out right now, it just might go off, hear?"

Stringer put his hat back on and got out his wallet. "Look, I'll show you my identification."

But she shoved the gun muzzle further out at him. "Don't bother. It's as easy to take an honest man's wallet as his watch, once you take to robbing folk."

He sighed in resignation, and put his wallet away. Then, as he began to turn as if to leave, he grabbed the muzzle of her shotgun and pulled hard . . . .

Also in the STRINGER series from Charter

STRINGER
STRINGER ON DEAD MAN'S RANGE
STRINGER ON THE ASSASSINS' TRAIL
STRINGER AND THE HANGMAN'S RODEO
STRINGER AND THE HANGING JUDGE
(coming in May)

LOU CAMERON

STRINGER

AND THE WILD BUNCH

CHARTER BOOKS, NEW YORK

STRINGER AND THE WILD BUNCH

A Charter Book/published by arrangement with
the author

PRINTING HISTORY
Charter edition/March 1988

ISBN: 1-55773-010-5

Charter Books are published by The Berkley Publishing Group,
200 Madison Avenue, New York, New York 10016.
The name "Charter" and the "C" logo are trademarks
belonging to Charter Communications, Inc.
PRINTED IN THE UNITED STATES OF AMERICA

10 9 8 7 6 5 4 3 2 1

CHAPTER
ONE

Stringer was thinking about robbing stagecoaches in Arizona when the Wild Bunch robbed the train he was riding in Colorado. So it took him a few seconds to figure out what was going on.

The train had just picked up some speed after a jerkwater stop on the west slope of the Divide when somebody yanked mighty hard on the emergency cord, locking every wheel of the U.P. Flyer. Stringer had been working at a writing table in the club car with a schooner of beer at his elbow and his notes spread out before him. So the sudden stop deposited a lot of beer and some of his notes in his lap. Fortunately he was wearing the faded denim jacket and jeans he favored in the field. But he was still cussing pretty good as he stood over the wet table in his wet jeans, trying to flatten beer-soaked paper on the glass top before it fell apart, when a portly old gent in a conductor's uniform tore through the front door of the club car. He ran the length of

1

it with surprising speed and grace, and vaulted the brass rail of the rear platform to land, still running, in the direction of that last stop.

Stringer and the other confused passengers in the club car were still staring after him when a trio of dusty desperadoes with feed sacks over their heads herded a colored porter ahead of them through the forward entrance. One of the masked men fired a round into the ceiling panels, filling the car with gun smoke and paint chips as he yelled, "This is a stick-up!"

Stringer and the other club car passengers had already guessed as much. Stringer's thoughts strayed wistfully to the gun rig he'd left packed in his gladstone up forward, in deference to his more sedately dressed fellow passengers. He decided it was just as well since he only had about thirty dollars on him at the moment, and any man who'd take on three armed men for thirty dollars had to be more stupid than daring.

One of the owlhoots who hadn't shot up the ceiling fanned at the smoke with his six-gun and announced in a more reasonable tone, "I don't know why he does that, neither. I'm sure you all know how this game is played. This here colored boy is fixing to pass his hat amongst you, and your protracted existence depends on how well you ante up."

As the porter moved down the aisle with his peaked cap inverted, the obvious leader of the trio peered toward the rear and added, "That don't include you, ma'am. We wouldn't have to ask these gents to contribute to our support if that greedy old Mr. Harriman who owns this railroad hadn't slickered us with a new safe in the baggage car up front. My pards may or may not manage to open her. Meanwhile, time's a wasting and we ain't about to ride on empty-handed."

Stringer knew better than to turn his head. He recalled the object of the bandit leader's admiration as a plain but not too ugly woman who'd been seated alone on the rear platform when he'd first sat down at the writing table. As he stood by it now, the porter got to him with the hat. Stringer shrugged, hauled out his billfold, and emptied it into the pot. The leader nodded in satisfaction. "I figured you for a top hand," he said. "How come you wet your jeans like that, old son? Ain't you never heard a gun go off afore?"

Stringer smiled thinly and replied, "It's beer. I wasn't expecting such a sudden stop just now."

The masked man chuckled inside his feed sack. "Having someone slip aboard at a jerkwater to jerk the brake line is a lot more scientific than felling trees across the track. It's a lot less work, too, come to study on it."

He started to move on. Then he spotted the wet paper spread on the glass tabletop near Stringer and reached with his free hand to pick a sheet up. Stringer snapped, "Don't! You'll only tear it!"

But the owlhoot paid him no mind until he'd picked up the corner of a soggy sheet, the corner tearing free of the page. "When you're right you're right, cowboy," he said. "What was you doing here, your homework? No offense, but you look sort of mature for a high school boy working stock on weekends."

Stringer had to be nice to the curious cuss. For despite the casual tone of the stick-up, one man was posted at the far end with a ferocious Lemat revolver and an unreadable expression on the burlap face he exposed to the world. So Stringer explained, "I'm a newspaper man. Until you boys showed up, I was on my way to interview Miss Pearl Hart for the *San Francisco Sun*. She just got out of prison, and my feature editor seems to feel she was some kind of bandit queen in her day."

The one who shot up ceilings had moved on down the line with the porter and his hat by now. But the friendlier leader seemed to find Stringer more interesting. He said, "Well, you still look sort of cow to me. But I recall the doings of Miss Pearl Hart a few years back. She sounds like my sort of woman, and they say she ain't bad looking, neither. It was the Globe Stage she robbed that time, right?"

Stringer nodded. "She didn't get far, and nobody was hurt. That's likely why she only got seven years for her part in the robbery, if you follow my drift."

The train robber chuckled. "I told you we was good at this." Then he saw what his sidekick was up to and called out, "I said to leave that lady be, Arkansas! You just go on and take that brooch back, ma'am. I wasn't funning when I said I don't pick on women and children."

Stringer felt it was safe, now, to follow the owlhoot's gaze. He saw that the old gal in the shapeless tan travel duster was indeed in possession of her rhinestone brooch once more. She was blushing like a schoolgirl as she nodded their way. "I'd already heard of your gallantry to ladies, Mr. Cassidy," she said. "I'm so glad to see the tales they tell of you are true."

The compliment didn't seem to go down as well as it was no doubt meant. The leader yanked his feed sack off with his free hand and a roar of hurt pride to demand, "I ain't Butch Cassidy or that prissy Sundance Kid you cruel-hearted woman!"

They could all see now that whoever he was, he needed a shave, had glandular eyes, a walrus moustache, and thinning close-cropped hair. "I will have you know, ma'am," he announced, "that you owe your very life and virtue to the one and original Kid Curry. Cassidy ain't leading the Wild Bunch no more. *I* am. And I'd better not hear any arguments about that, hear?"

He glared at Stringer, who said nothing until Kid Curry demanded, "Would you be kind enough to put that in your fool paper for me, newspaper boy?"

"If you want me to," Stringer replied. "Whether I'll be reporting it as your capture or daring escape depends a lot on how much time you boys are giving yourselves. It's been a spell since the conductor of this train lit out for help, and I feel sure they have a telegraph at that jerkwater stop back yonder."

Kid Curry scowled thoughtfully, then nodded. "I fear you have a point, pilgrim. I have been waiting on the dulcet tones of a blown safe all the while we've been having this interesting conversation. But my boys tell me them new Mosler safes are a caution to open with nitro because of the sneaky way they made the doors. Do you know how to blow a Mosler, seeing as you're so interested in bandit queens and all?"

Stringer smiled incredulously. "I only write crime features. But if it's any comfort, I do recall reading about the Mosler patent. They've got a sort of groove just inside the crack that lets the nitro all run down and out as fast as a yegg man can pack it in, right?"

Kid Curry shrugged. "If you say so. We'd have heard by now if my boys had figured some way to blow the fool box, so we'd best ride on. We brung plenty of spare mounts. Put on your sombrero and let's go, newspaper boy."

Stringer blinked in dismay. "What are you talking about? You got all my money, and my paper's not about to pay any ransom for me, if that's what you have in mind."

Kid Curry shook his bullet head. "I ain't out to kidnap

nobody. That ain't my style, neither. I'm simply the best old train robber in the world, and it's about time the world knew it. So you're coming along to hear my sad story and see that every word gets printed true. I'm getting sick and tired of Butch and Sundance getting all the credit for my efforts in these parts, hear?"

There were more like a dozen in the gang, all told, once Kid Curry had his followers and the bemused Stringer mounted up and riding north through mighty rough country. Stringer had naturally brought his old Rough Rider hat along. The others had exchanged their feed sacks for various types of battered broad brims. But Kid Curry favored a brown derby that might have seemed a mite more dapper if it hadn't sported a bullet hole through its crown.

Stringer didn't ask where they were headed. He'd heard many a tale of the Hole in the Wall country. He knew that in the direction they seemed to be headed, they'd wind up in rough country soon.

It was bad enough already. Stringer was gaining a grudging respect for Kid Curry's choice of time and place as he noticed the shadows were already lengthening. They were leaving plenty of sign as they bulled through second-growth aspen and the alder hells choking the low draws they roller-coasted over at a most uncomfortable but mile-eating trot. Stringer knew that by the time the posse gathered back there along the track in enough strength to risk pursuit, it would be dark. So even if the law felt frisky enough to chase a good-sized gang into the tall timber in tricky light, they'd likely just get lost. Stringer knew his old pal Charlie Siringo, and the less likable but no less canny Joe Lefors had been spearheading the hunt for the Wild Bunch this season. Stringer wasn't sure he wanted to be this close to any member of the Wild Bunch when, not if, the law caught up with them. An aspen trunk snagged his right stirrup, and while he had no trouble freeing it, he noted the white gash he'd left in the gray-green birchlike bark. He resisted the temptation to blaze a helpful trail. Charlie Siringo wouldn't need his help, and the moody Deputy Marshal Lefors tended to shoot at every moving critter in sight. Stringer felt his own best bet would be not to be anywhere near these galoots any longer than he had to be. Meanwhile it was still too light to even consider making a break for it.

But Stringer was making mental notes of the few handy landmarkers amid the tangle of brush and saplings all around, when Kid Curry fell in beside him to opine, "You ride pretty good for a gent with such a sissy job. Tell me some more about yourself, old son."

Stringer shrugged and reached for the makings of a Bull Durham smoke. "There's not all that much to tell. I was birthed in the Mother Lode country as Stuart MacKail. They call me Stringer now because that's what I do for the *San Francisco Sun*. I'm a stringer or free-lance writer for 'em. Since I grew up on a cow spread and worked my way through college punching cows, old Sam Barca, my features editor, likes to send me out on stories about the wild west, or what's left of it."

"Well, you'll find her wild enough where we're all headed," Kid Curry said. "Once we get up around the headwaters of the Green, I'll show you country so wild it ain't on no map. It's a pure lie that Butch Cassidy found the Hole in the Wall country. The first outlaws of any import up around Billings was the Red Sash Gang and they was even before *my* time."

Stringer frowned thoughtfully but continued to roll his Bull Durham. "Jesus, are we on our way to *Montana?*"

Kid Curry laughed. "Not hardly. That was where the

Hole in the Wall story got started. After the law had it sort of located in the hills west of Billings, the old boys took to working out of a dry deserted stretch of Wyoming. Once the law had *that* mapped as the Hole in the Wall, we sort of moved her to the headwaters of the Green on this side of the Divide. It's just dumb to have a hideout the law knows about, you see."

Stringer licked his cigarette paper to seal it. "I'm commencing to follow your drift. A Pinkerton man I know once told me he doubted there was any particular place you boys had a hole in any wall to ride through. His name was Charlie Siringo. Have you heard of him, Kid?"

Kid Curry shrugged. "I got too many lawmen hunting me to keep track of all their fool names. Is this old pal of your'n likely to be trailing us right now? If he is, I sure hope you ain't too fond of him. What kind of a name is Siringo, anyhow? He sounds like a dago."

Stringer flared a match with his thumbnail and lit his smoke before he replied, "I think he's Irish-Italian. Whatever he may be, old Charlie's Texas-bred and hasn't lost a gunfight yet. I sort of hope it's him they'll send after us. Siringo's sort of firm but fair. If we run into Joe Lefors . . ."

"Him I know," Kid Curry cut in with a growl. "You're right about him being mean. But he's dumb as hell as well. Me and the boys has been having lots of fun with him and that fancy railroad posse of his. Old Mr. Harriman's given 'em a private railroad car to ride about in after us. They even have their fool horses riding first class up and down the U.P. line. How on earth do you reckon they figure on catching anyone like that?"

Stringer took a drag on his smoke and said, "Oh, I reckon they mean to just keep trying. They wouldn't have those horses riding with them if they meant to confine all their searching for you to the tracks, Kid."

Curry snorted in disgust. "Well, there ain't no railroad tracks or even trails where we're all headed right now. Once we bust outten this timber we won't be leaving half as much sign for the bastards, neither. I'm glad you ride so good, Stringer. We got us some slick-rock riding ahead and I'd hate to lose you off a cliff afore you could write down my sad story for the world to read. Some of the mean things they say about me just ain't fair."

"Are they true?" asked Stringer, since he'd heard some things about Kid Curry in his travels that were sort of alarming.

The owlhoot made a wry face and replied, "True or false, you newspaper rascals have a way of twisting words to make a man look badder than he may be. What does High Stairable mean? That's what someone writ I was, and he wasn't even there when I gunned that saddle tramp for spilling hot coffee on me that time. I wasn't High Stairable when I kilt him. I was scalded. Wouldn't you gun a fool who poured hot coffee on you, pard?"

"I might see if he had anything to say about being sorry first," Stringer said.

"Not if the coffee was really hot," Kid Curry insisted. "When a man scalds me, I don't care if he's sorry or not. The point is that I wasn't High Stairable at the time. I just riz to my feet, smiling reasonable, and announced my intent to all assembled. It was his own damn fault he was slow on the draw for a man who thought it was funny to pour hot coffee over folk. You know he was still grinning when I shot him?"

"He may not have understood how serious the situation was," Stringer said. "I think the word you're groping for might be hysterical."

Kid Curry said, "I ain't that, neither. You'll find that I'm as friendly a cuss as you might ever want to meet, as long as you don't do nothing to upset me. I want you to tell everybody they printed the name of that rascal I shot all wrong."

Stringer asked what the victim's right name might really be.

Kid Curry shrugged. "Hell, how should I know? He was just a saddle tramp who drifted in one day, telling Butch and the others tall tales about all the wonders he'd seen and done. I could tell right off he was just talk. Nobody else believed me until I showed 'em all how slow he was on the draw. My point is that he wasn't a famous owlhoot, like that reporter said. Nobody but a total idiot would fight with his real pards unless he had to. Them stories about me and Sundance not getting along is pure bull. Why, I backed old Butch and Sundance the time they drummed Harry Tracy out of the Wild Bunch. It was Sundance as told Tracy to ride on. But I would have shot him if he'd stood up to old Sundance. He likely knowed it. So he left without no fuss and—"

"Hold it," Stringer cut in. "Are we talking about the Harry Tracy who terrorized the whole northwest a summer or so ago?"

Kid Curry nodded. "Sundance said he was loco en la cabeza. That's why we didn't want him riding with us. He even shot his own pard, Dave Merril, in a dirty duel. They'd agreed to slap leather on the count of ten, and old Harry drew on the count of seven. Worse yet, old Harry killed himself, later, when the law had him pinned down. How's that for High Stairable?"

Stringer sighed. "Harry Tracy was a sort of moody cuss, as I look back on it. That was one of the first Stateside stories I covered after getting back from the Alaska gold rush. In fairness to a graduate of the Wild Bunch, however, be it recorded that when Harry Tracy chose to blow his own brains out, he'd been shot up considerable by rifle fire. He had a busted leg and a shattered right arm, so—"

"It was still a crazy-yellow way to act," Kid Curry cut in, adding, "Suicide is a mortal sin. It says so in the Good Book."

Stringer didn't think the high-strung killer he was riding with wanted to discuss the other commandments. So he neither mentioned them nor asked how many the present leader of the Wild Bunch might have broken in his time. But that reminded him of other questions that might be of interest to his readers, if he ever got out of this mess alive, so he asked in a desperately casual voice if they might be meeting up with Butch or Sundance somewhere up ahead.

Kid Curry shook his head. "Not hardly. They're both acting sort of mysterious right now. Sundance had to go east on family business a spell back. He hails from New Jersey. I don't know why Butch went with him, or even if Butch did. Some say old Butch is down in Texas right now. Anyway, the rest of us still got to eat. So that's how come I'm sort of in command at the moment."

Since the odds on anyone else making more sense were good, Stringer asked if any other members of the Wild Bunch were sort of disputing Kid Curry's leadership at the moment.

The pop-eyed owlhoot looked away and then explained, "Most of the boys are democrats. If they wasn't sort of prone to think for themselves, they'd be herding cows or sacking feed for some regular boss. It just ain't true that the Wild Bunch is some sort of infernal lodge with infernal rules and regulations. Suffice it to say I'm the boss of this here chapter of the Wild Bunch, and I'll be vexed as hell if you don't obey my every command."

Stringer saw no good reason yet to express his own reservations on that point. He was riding a strange mount, unarmed, and not too sure where to run if and when he got the chance to make a break for it. The low sun to their west told him which way north and south might be. He knew they were somewhere north of the main U.P. line. After that it was up for grabs. They'd been hairpinning through the sort of country that gave the Rocky Mountains their name, and it would surely be dark before he could get anywhere important.

As if he'd been thinking along the same lines, Kid Curry said, "We'll be holing up for the night soon. Do you figure we'll have to tie you up after supper, old son?"

Stringer grimaced. "I didn't know that was for me to say."

"The boys will be expecting me to," Kid Curry said. "Unless I can say I have your parole."

Stringer didn't answer. He'd been raised cow by folk who took a man's word serious, and while he'd seen more of this old wicked world than his more rustic relations, he still hated to break his word, unless he had to.

Kid Curry waited, grinned slyly, and said, "That ain't gonna work, Stringer. You can consider yourself my prisoner and get treated the same way or you can give me your word and be my bathwash."

Stringer had to think some about that. Then he laughed. "Don't you mean your Boswell?"

Kid Curry said, "I mean that friendly Scotchman who rid with Doc Johnson and writ down all them nice things about him so's the world would never forget him. It wouldn't have been modest for Doc Johnson to write all them nice things about himself, see?"

Stringer laughed again. "Let's see if I have this straight," he replied. "You want me to interview you on the fly and turn in a favorable review on your activities?"

Kid Curry nodded. "Just like that writer Bathwash done. I read a piece on me in the *Denver Post* a spell back that almost made me cry blood. It just ain't fair to make up such mean things about a poor boy who never had a chance, see?"

Stringer tried to keep a sober expression as he replied, "I feel sure you're as decent, way down deep, as say Jesse James or Billy the Kid must have been. But just how am I supposed to submit your biography to my features editor unless you boys turn me loose sooner or later?"

Kid Curry looked as sincere as your average habitual criminal as he told Stringer, "We got some riding to do afore we're clear of the fuss we just stirred up back yonder. Once we're up in the Hole in the Wall and I have time to study on what you want to put in the papers about me, I may even give you your money back."

Then he said, more ominously, "Of course, if I don't like what you put down about me—"

"That's the only thing neither of us has to worry about," Stringer quickly cut in. "I used to write advertisements when I was starting out as a journalist. You can't be harder to sell than soft soap or rat poison."

Curry scowled at him uncertainly, and Stringer made a mental note that dry humor was not one of the ruffian's stronger points. Curry's tone was less certain than his words when he said, "There you go. You treat me right and I'll treat you right. Do we have us a deal?"

Stringer hesitated before nodding. "With one line of small print. I can see you and I seem to get along tolerable. But what if some of the others, well, spill hot coffee on me?"

"They won't," Kid Curry said. "If they know what's good for 'em. I'll spread the word you're my guest. You can't have no gun. I ain't that stupid. But otherwise, the usual camp rules apply. So you have my permit to say no if somebody wants to corn-hole you, and if anybody hits you, I reckon it's all right for you to hit him or her back."

"Him or *her?*" Stringer asked.

Kid Curry grinned. "We got plenty of her-critters hiding out with us up to the headwaters of the Green. I said we was mostly democrats, not a bunch of queers. I'll fix you up with one of the gals, once we get there. It ain't true that Sundance's woman, old Etta Place, is the only good-looking gal who ever pined for a life of romantic adventure!"

Curry laughed almost boyishly and added, "Stick with me, and I'll show you a right good time, newspaper boy." Then he sort of took the edge off his words of cheer by warning, "Make a break for it afore I tell you I won't mind, and I'll likely blow your kneecaps off and leave you staked face up across an ant pile. That's what I done to the last son of a bitch who tried to double-cross me, hear?"

CHAPTER
TWO

A pale moon was rising above the inky ridges to their east, just in time, when Kid Curry led them all across an open stretch of loose scree. None of their mounts left hoofprints in the fist-sized lumps of frost-shattered granite. Their mounts had enough trouble trying not to slide on down the mountain. Stringer rode with a gentle hand on his own mount's reins. He knew all he could do if the brute lost its footing was to try and fall on the high side and hope for the best. The scree they were dislodging with every hoof step made ominous noises as it rattled down, down and down some more into the mysterious darkness below. A million or so years later they'd made it to the far side, which would have seemed a lot nicer if the far side of the loose scree hadn't consisted of bare bedrock sloping almost thirty degrees to an even steeper drop-off.

Kid Curry didn't feel as sure of the route he'd chosen as he acted. He waited until they were all on firmer ground in the trees to the north before he let out his breath with a wheeze and declared, "I'd like to see the law cross that stretch of asshole pucker in broad day."

Another owlhoot laughed and said, "We ain't left a hoof mark for the last couple of miles, and for that they'll surely thank you, Kid. You sure are a fool for ridge running, and nobody but a fool like me would consider riding after you and the other mountain goats."

Kid Curry announced he was slicker than any mountain goat, and led them on. Stringer saw no indication they were following even a game trail as they wound through brooding fir and moonlit outcrops of rounded granite. He'd heard there was an unmapped outlaw trail running all the way down to Mexico between the more or less north-south ranges west of the Divide. But he didn't see how this could be it. He could only hope Kid Curry wasn't lost. He knew *he* was, and unless someone was starting to unscrew the stars up yonder, they were due for some rain before moon-set.

He didn't say so. Some of the others seemed uncertain of his status, to judge from occasional growls he heard, and he was now riding in the middle of the single-file column as they snaked on along the contour line of the steep east-west slope, with the only man who'd talk nice to him well out front.

The stars were gone and the moon was shining mighty dim by the time they heard roaring rapids ahead and reined in by a white-water stream. Kid Curry shot a thoughtful glance up at the sky and announced, "It's already raining up in the Rabbit Ear ranges. Come morning they'll play hell finding hoof mark one in these parts. But we'd best play fox and hounds with the bastards whilst we have the chance. We'll wade down a ways afore we cross over."

"Don't you mean, *up*, Kid?" one of his followers protested. "I agreed to rob trains with you, not to commit suicide. Our ponies might make her upstream against that considerable current. But riding downstream is just asking 'em to lose their footing, with the water this high."

"Let's hope the posse shares your gloom, Arkansas," Kid Curry replied. "Given a fifty-fifty choice, assuming they trail us this far, they'll likely head upstream instead of downstream. That's why we're heading down, see?"

Then, without waiting for an argument, Kid Curry rode into the almost stirrup-deep white water and, sure enough, headed down the mountain with moonlit foam washing halfway up his pony's rump. After some cussing, all but one of the others followed. Stringer understood why one independent thinker chose to head upstream, alone. But he didn't feel Kid Curry would understand if *he* headed that way. So he headed downstream as well. It was a good thing he was a good rider. In no time at all he and his mount were in trouble. The pony's steel-shod hooves kept slipping on the slick submerged rocks neither of them could see. It was only by shifting his weight in the saddle skillfully that Stringer managed to keep them both more or less upright, because the poor brute's rump was a lot higher than its forequarters, even when it wasn't slipping and sliding, with the current trying to move them a lot faster.

Things got worse before they got better. The mountain stream ran faster where it pinched between a stretch of steeper banks. Stringer almost lost his hat to a tree branch. More than one now lay in wait above the rolling water. It was tempting to duck low and stay there. But he knew a rider with his belly to the horn would have a time shifting his weight enough to matter. So he only ducked under the thicker branches and pushed the others out of the way with his free hand. Once he saved both himself and his mount from a ducking by hanging on hard when the pony put a hoof down wrong. Then they were steady again, or as steady as horse and rider could be on such treacherous footing.

Stringer heard a cry of anguish behind him and yanked hard on the reins to halt and brace his own mount for what might be coming. It was a near thing when another pony bumped into them, floating and flailing, to bounce off and continue downstream, its wet saddle empty. As the spilled rider passed, making even more noise, Stringer let go his reins, grabbed an overhead branch with one hand, and just managed to snag the man's shirt with the other hand. The panic-stricken owlhoot grabbed Stringer's free arm in both hands and hung on for dear life, coughing and retching.

"I got you, damn it," Stringer said. "If I wanted to go swimming with you, I'd say so. See if you can hook a foot with mine in the stirrup and I'll try to haul you up aboard this bronc."

The half-drowned rascal did as he was told. It wasn't easy. He was the skinny consumptive they called Slim, and he was no stronger than he looked. But after considerable cussing, Slim was sort of sitting sidesaddle on Stringer's lap.

"I don't know about you," Stringer said, "but I've had enough of this fool creek."

Slim agreed, and together, they worked their mutual mount up the bank. They wound up on the far side, at least, but Kid Curry still might have objected had not a couple of the others followed Stringer's example. Kid Curry must not have wanted to ride all the way to the Grand Canyon alone, for he rode up out of the wild water as well, calling out, "When you're right you're right. Ain't you glad, now, I didn't tie that old boy's hands like you thought I should, Slim?"

The wet and shivering Slim slid down from his awkward perch on Stringer's wet jeans. "I owe you one, newspaper boy," he said. "For this other crazy bastard must think I'm a damned old trout, and he knows I got delicate lungs."

One of the others led a spare mount over and told the soaking-wet lunger, "I hope you didn't have nothing you value aboard that pony you was riding, Slim. It's long gone, even if it ain't drownded by now. Get aboard this old mare and try not to fall off no more."

Slim mounted up. "I never fell off nothing," he protested, "damn your eyes. Was it my fault that gelding decided to go swimming underwater like a damned old pearl diver?"

"All right, we've had our fun," Kid Curry said. "Now we'd best move on."

So they did. Stringer felt even more turned around as he saw they were headed more west than north now. They still seemed to be following a cross-slope contour line. He squinted at the mental map of the Rockies he'd thought he had in his head. He saw he wasn't the only one who didn't know these hills as well as he'd thought when another rider asked Kid Curry where in the hell they were going.

Their leader called back, "Hole in the Wall, the easy way. We got us the Rabbit Ears due north, and I just hate to be riding above timberline with the law on my ass. That's how come we got to go around instead of over, see?"

Someone else protested, "I just caught me a raindrop with my hat brim, and I'm already wet enough from that fool creek, Kid."

"Don't break out your slickers, boys," Kid Curry replied. "I told you all when we started out that I knowed this country good. Stick with me and I'll have you warm and dry in no time."

It was more like an hour, and the rain was coming down

hard enough to force everyone but Stringer and the unfortunate Slim into their slickers by the time Kid Curry called out, "Here we are. What did I tell you?"

Since it was now almost pitch-dark, more than one of the other train robbers demanded to know what in thunder he was talking about. Kid Curry dismounted. "Stay put whilst I shed some light on the subject. The clay footing around here is sort of treachersome when it's this wet."

They all waited in the dark rain until they saw Kid framed in what seemed at first a doorway. Then they realized he'd lit an oil lantern in the adit of a mine, and it shed light on the wet mud all around. So they quickly dismounted and led their mounts closer. Stringer swore as his boot heel slipped on banana-peel wet clay. Kid Curry had been right about that too.

They led the ponies in under the low overhang. As he tied his to a mine timber, Stringer saw Kid Curry had joined him. "I give up," he said. "If this isn't the Hole in the Wall, what is it?"

"Gold mine," Kid Curry said. "A fool's gold mine at least. From the looks of her, she was dug back in the sixties or seventies. Whoever dug her gave up years ago, but the timbers still look sound. Don't go too far back, though. Ground water's rotted the timbers a ways in, and I'd hate to lose you now. How do you like my story so far?"

"You're good," Stringer said, truthfully enough. "I don't know how the hell you could have planned on this rain to wash away all sign of your sins, and you must be half owl as well."

Kid Curry frowned. "Are you saying I got funny eyes?"

Stringer assured him his eyes looked just fine. "I'm glad to hear that," Curry said. "My dear old mother had sort of poppy eyes, too, and we always thought she was pretty. Whether I take after her or not, nobody but Sundance is allowed to make fun of my poppy eyes, and that's only because he's the only man I know who can draw half as fast as me. I've got to see about getting us a good fire going now. None of the others has a lick of sense, and I have to tell 'em when to eat and shit."

Stringer didn't argue. He unsaddled his mount and rubbed it as dry as he could manage with a damp saddle blanket. It wasn't for him to say whether the poor brute got watered and fed. He moved deeper into the mine and found a dusty dynamite box to sit on as he watched some of the others trying to build a fire even deeper, with damp matches and considerable cussing. Stringer reached absently for his makings, felt how they were in his soaked-through shirt, and decided it wasn't worth the effort. His tobacco and papers might be dry enough to smoke by sunrise, if they ever got that fire going.

He knew his own matches were supposed to be waterproof. So he rose, ambled over, and hunkered down by the one called Arkansas. Arkansas had busted a mess of damp matches to no avail. But when Stringer offered to try, Arkansas seemed to take this as a personal insult. He'd been the one aboard the train who liked to shoot at ceilings, Stringer recalled. So he kept his own voice calmer and more reasonable as he explained, "I'm not saying you don't know how to build a fire, Arkansas. Anyone can see how fine you shaved that kindling. It's just that, no offense, your matches are wet. I got some here made Mexican style out of wax."

Someone else said, "Let him try, at least. I got goose bumps on my goose bumps, and anyone can see you and your matches are both all wet, Arkansas."

There was a chorus of agreement. So before Arkansas could outright tell him not to, Stringer struck a light and thrust it into the kindling. "There you go," he said as it caught fire. "I told you I admired your shaved kindling, old son."

As the others softly cheered, Arkansas scowled like the overgrown schoolyard bully he probably was. "I ain't your son or any relation to you, you bastard. My mother and father married lawsome afore they had me."

Stringer let that go unchallenged. He had no other choice, since his own gun was miles away in a gladstone, while Arkansas was wearing a brace of double-action Colt Lightnings. Hoping it didn't count when a man who called you a bastard had the drop on you, Stringer edged back from the fire, braced his back against the damp rock wall of the shaft, and saw that Arkansas had apparently forgiven or forgotten him in his eagerness to hog the fire closer than anyone with live ammo around his waist and a lick of sense might have wanted to.

Another gang member produced a tin bucket and some provisions to put on the fire, and as the dank interior of the deserted mine warmed up, the mulligan commenced to boil and smell a lot more tempting than it looked going into the pot. Stringer hadn't been thinking about supper, up to now. But he was suddenly aware he'd missed it aboard that fool train. Had things gone less exciting, he'd have likely eaten hours ago and been in his Pullman berth by now, with or without that gal he'd noticed traveling alone.

Kid Curry came over and sat down beside Stringer. "I just checked out front," he said. "We ain't casting enough light out the adit to worry about. It faces an old stamp mill across the way, and we're down in a draw to begin with. Do you want to start writing about me now, or would you rather wait until we grub?"

"That mulligan has some boiling to go," Stringer said, "if that was jerky I saw 'em toss in just now. But I don't have my notebook or even a pencil on me at the moment."

The pop-eyed owlhoot swore and bawled out, "Hey, do any of you boys have a pencil?"

"Never mind," Stringer soothed. "I only need to make notes of names, dates, and places. Why don't you just tell me how you got started in this business, and we can get her down on paper in the sweet by and by?"

Kid Curry nodded and began. "I was raised in Missouri, the same as Frank and Jesse James, and brought up decent by kind parents, the same as they was. But you know how hard it was on us all during the infernal Reconstruction, so—"

"Hold it," Stringer cut in, explaining, "My readers just won't buy that, no offense. President Rutherford Hayes ended the mayhaps fair or unfair treatment of ex-Confederates way back in 1876. So while the James and Younger brothers may or may not have had just call to resent the Reconstruction, you'd have just been learning to talk about the time Johnny Reb and Damnyankee became dead issues."

Kid Curry shook his derbied head. "You wouldn't think that if you'd been raised in our part of Missouri. I lost my cherry afore I knew Damnyankee might be said as two words. You ain't no Damnyankee, are you?"

Stringer said, "We called ourselves Californianos. But for the record, I was roping top-hand before someone told me Robert E. Lee wasn't just a steamboat. I'll say you were driven desperate by the Lost Cause if that's the way you want it. What happened next?"

"Folk picked on us," Curry almost whined. "I wasn't imagining it. I had me three brothers, and they can tell you they was picked on too. Two of my brothers turned out as mean as me after all that picking on, back home."

"What happened to your other brother?" Stringer asked.

Curry sighed. "He must have been the sissy of the family. So far, he ain't never been in trouble with the law. But never mind about my Missouri kin. I left there early, after I had to gun an uppity old boy who kept picking on me. I come out west, hoping to leave all that trouble ahind me. But I dunno, it seems everywhere I go, folk pick on me. I lost a job in Texas when I had to shoot a foreman who said I was lazy. I shot another man in Dodge for calling me pop-eyed. Then I sort of fell in with old George Curry and—"

"Hold it," Stringer cut in. "Are we talking about the one and original Flat Nose Curry, best remembered for shooting it out with a Utah posse near Thompson Springs a few years back?"

"He was one of the founding fathers of the Wild Bunch," Curry replied, "and he taught me everything I know."

Stringer grimaced. "What was he to you, an uncle or something?"

It took Kid Curry a moment to catch his meaning. "Hell, my real name ain't Curry. I was baptized Harvey Logan. They took to calling me Kid Curry because old George sort of treated me like his kid. My brothers, Johnny and Lonny, still go by the name of Logan. You'll be meeting up with 'em if we don' get cut off by the law betwixt here and Brown's Hole."

Stringer swore under his breath. "You were right. I'm going to need a pencil and paper. I might be able to remember Butch Cassidy is really named Parker, and you just told me your real name is Logan. But how in the hell did someone named Brown get into this discussion?"

Kid Curry frowned. "*I* don't have no trouble keeping things straight. The first Hole in the Wall was up near Billings. Then the law found out about her and we moved it to a cliffed-in valley closer to Casper, Wyoming. Then we had to set up in old Star Valley on the Wyoming-Idaho line. Some sneaky range detectives found out about Star Valley, so we've been working out of Brown's Hole, where the borders of Colorado, Wyoming, and Utah meet around the headwaters of the Green, like I told you before. Ain't you been paying me no mind at all?"

"I've been trying to," Stringer said. "It's not easy. In other words, such places as the Hole in the Wall or Robber's Roost are wherever you boys feel they ought to be at the moment, right?"

"Don't talk dumb," Kid Curry said. "Everybody knows Robber's Roost is a mesa in southeast Utah. That's where Butch Cassidy got his name. He started out riding with Big Mike Cassidy, who raises cows in Mexico these days. All us young gents devoted to free enterprise have to learn the ropes from older and wiser owlhoots. A boy just started out on his own is sure to get caught. Didn't you know that?"

Stringer smiled thinly. "I suspected as much when I decided to put myself through college after I got tired of the beef industry. The more I listen to you, the surer I am that I made the right choice. I don't see how I could get your business straight in my head with an older mentor teaching me from textbooks on the subject."

Kid Curry shrugged. "Well, to tell the truth, we like to confuse outsiders about such matters as our real names and current addresses. Just call me Kid Curry in that story you're fixing to write about me, and forget where we might be while you get it down right. I don't know where in the hell we'd move to if the law found out where the Hole in the Wall is right now."

Stringer offered no suggestions. Someone announced the mulligan was as ready as it was likely to get, and Stringer lost track of Kid Curry in the general stampede. Stringer thought it wiser to stay put and let the gents with guns eat first. After a while he got a crack at the pot, filled a tin cup, and moved deeper into the mine to consume it. He found a slab of fallen rock just about right for sitting on. He got out his pocket knife to use as a spear for the bigger lumps. As he got the first chunk of not-bad stewed jerky in his mouth and proceeded to chew hell out of it, an angry voice snapped, "Hey, how come you got a weapon concealed on you, prisoner?"

It was the one called Arkansas. Stringer wasn't surprised. For who else would have followed him so far from the fire just to ask dumb questions?

Stringer looked up, swallowed, and said, "I don't know what you might call a weapon, amigo, but where I come from, this is a bitty jackknife. I'm sorry if it makes you nervous. Why don't you go someplace else and let me worry about stabbing my fool self to death with it as I inhale this mulligan?"

Arkansas smiled down at him like a buzzard who'd just spied a lamb lost on a salt flat. "Well, now," he purred, "don't we talk brave for a newspaper dude who likely has to squat to piss? How come you're so brave, newspaper boy? Do you really think you could take a real man?"

Stringer shrugged. "I don't know. I don't see any around here. Where I come from, real men don't rawhide unarmed gents when they're packing a brace of double-actions."

"Are you saying mean things about the proud state of Arkansas, you Californee pansy?"

"It's California poppies we're famous for," Stringer said. "I can't say I know your state well enough to insult or praise it. But if you're trying to make me admire it, you're doing a piss-poor job. Maybe you'd feel better if you went to jerk off somewhere else, Arkansas. You know I can't fight you. So your war dance is just a waste of time."

Arkansas blinked in surprise. Then he scowled and roared, "I'll show you a war dance, you smartass fancy Dan! I'll show you how we stomp piss ants like you in Arkansas or anywhere's else we finds them!"

He might have. Stringer was tensed to roll out of the way, even though he doubted he could avoid bullets as well as boots. Then another voice called out, "Leave him alone, Arkansas."

They both turned to see it was Slim. The skinny consumptive had dried out some by now, but he still looked pale and shiversome as he moved closer down the mine shaft.

Arkansas laughed. "What's this dude to you, Slim? You don't look healthy enough to fuck nobody this evening."

"You're right," Slim said. "I feel sick as hell. I'd feel even worse if Stringer hadn't hauled me outten that creek back there. So I want you to leave him alone. I don't mean to say that again."

Arkansas laughed, incredulous. "I don't take orders from no walking skeleton, and it's for me to say who I might or might not want to rawhide, see?"

Slim nodded, and though his hand didn't make any giveaway move near the tie-down holster down his right thigh, he sounded serious enough when he said, "All right. Fill your fist, if that's your pleasure."

Arkansas gasped. "You can't mean that, Slim," he protested. "You and me are pards. We got no call to fight over a damned outsider!"

"You're wrong," Slim said. "I got plenty of call to fight you, Arkansas. I don't like you. I never have. You're a blowhard and a bully. You'd have to grow up with my frail constitution to know how much I've always hated bullies. Since I've learned to use a gun, I've sort of got over being scared of bullies. But I still dislike 'em considerable. So do you aim to draw or crawfish? I don't give a shit either way."

Arkansas gulped. "Hell, I can't fight you, Slim. Even if I could, can't you see me and old Stringer was just funning?"

Slim stared soberly down at Stringer. "It's for you to say, Stringer. I told you I owed you. So do you want to say the two of you was just funning or do you want this silly son of a bitch dead?"

"Let it go, Slim," Stringer said. "I don't mind an old boy saying he aims to stomp me, as long as he hasn't done it yet."

Slim shrugged. "I want you on the far side of the fire now," he told Arkansas. "If I catch you rawhiding this gent again, I'll slap leather on you sure as hell."

Arkansas turned and walked away, making brave noises under his breath. Slim told Stringer to let him know if anyone started up with him again.

"I'd say we're even now," Stringer said. "I don't want you getting in trouble on my account."

"I've been in trouble for some time," Slim replied. "The doc said my lungs might heal up in this thin mountain air. But it don't seem to be working. I ain't worried about no other kind of trouble. Arkansas ain't as yellow as you might think. He's seen me draw."

"I figured you had that sort of rep," Stringer said. "But what do you reckon Kid Curry would do or say if you took to gunning members of his gang on my account?"

Slim shrugged. "The Kid would know better than to do anything. He's seen me draw too. As for saying anything about it, he knows I'm worth Arkansas and his mother to the gang, even if his mother screws good. We just brung Arkansas along to let him get some practice. Kid Curry knows who's just noise and who he can count on in a pinch."

"Can he count on you in a pinch, Slim?"

"Don't try nothing funny, and we won't have to study on it. I was on my way back here to warn you that we've been sort of wondering about you. Kid Curry says you've given your parole. That may be good enough for him. What I was coming back here to tell you was that me or someone else will surely shoot you if you try to slip past the fire afore sunrise."

"Why, Slim, I thought you and me were friends."

"I ain't got no friends. I said I owed you, and I've been looking for an excuse to gun that other silly bastard."

CHAPTER
THREE

Falling asleep in damp duds on solid rock wasn't easy. So it seemed to Stringer he'd barely got there when someone nudged him awake. The fire had been allowed to go out. But there was just enough daylight coming down the shaft from the adit for him to make out the dim figure hunkered over him. He had to wait until it spoke some more to figure it was Kid Curry. The owlhoot said, "Slim seems in a bad way. Do you know anything about the doctor business, seeing as you're so educated?"

Stringer sat up and rubbed at his sleep-gummed eyes. "They failed to tell us much about TB in English Lit. But from what I've read on the subject since Dr. Koch discovered the bug a few years ago, a night in a damp mine after a frolic in a mountain stream would not be the treatment I'd prescribe."

Kid Curry nodded. "Rain's stopped and the sun's up. We'll spread a blanket on the grass and let Slim bake a spell. His poor spells seem to come and go. He'll likely feel better in a while. Meanwhile he's too sick to ride on, so I'm leaving you and some of the other boys here with Slim as the rest of us ride on."

Stringer didn't ask why. It would have been stupid to protest a lack of medical skills while Kid Curry was dealing him such a better hand. He got stiffly to his feet and followed Curry out of the mine. The sun was still low but it still hurt his eyes at first. As they adjusted to the morning glare, he saw that while all the ponies were tethered to abandoned machinery just outside, the human members of the gang had assembled on the grassy sunlit slope to the north. As the two of them crossed the sterile mud that paved the floor of the small secluded valley, Stringer saw that, sure enough, old Slim was spread out on one blanket, with another blanket spread over him. Seeing Slim asleep or unconscious, Stringer didn't ask the lunger how he felt that morning.

The small fire someone had kindled where the mud met the grass had gone out, or been put out. As Stringer and Kid Curry joined the group, a short, shy, or sullen rider they called Pecos handed Stringer a tomato can filled with black coffee. It was half cold and bitter as bile. But it seemed just the thing for sweeping cobwebs from a man's skull. Stringer thanked Pecos, who turned away without answering and moved up the slope a ways. There, he hunkered down in the damp grass and scowled at the world from under the brim of his big black hat.

Kid Curry indicated two other gents. "I want you to stay here with Banger, Will, and Pecos," he said, "till Slim dies or gets better. Pecos knows the trail, and you ought to be able to catch up with us. I don't think the law knows about this place. But since they can't be more than a day or so ahind us, I wouldn't give Slim more than one day in the sun if I was you. If he ain't better by sundown, another night in that mine will kill him for sure. So use your own judgment."

Stringer didn't argue. But as Kid Curry turned away, the one called Banger rose to follow him back down to the horses. Though Stringer couldn't make out their words, they seemed to be having a heated discussion. Kid Curry ended it by turning to call out, *"Vamanos, muchachos. There'll be time to rest up with strong liquor and weak-willed women where the rest of us are going."*

The ones who hadn't been told to stay rose, laughing or moaning, in accordance with how much sleep they'd had, and in a little while they'd all mounted up and ridden up the valley out of sight.

Banger came back from where the remaining ponies still stood sort of lonesome and threw himself down in the grass near Slim. "I don't like this. We'd agreed not to split up this time."

His sidekick, Will, sitting cross-legged on the far side of Slim's blanket, nodded. "That's how they caught up with the Tall Texan, got Deaf Charlie kilt, and scared Butch so bad we ain't seen him since. Nothing like that would have happened if they'd all stuck together after stopping old Engine Number Three."

Stringer chose a position between Slim's blanket and the shy or sullen Pecos. He reached for his makings and found that while they were still a mite damp, they'd dried enough to risk building a soggy smoke. As he did so, he asked Pecos what all of them were talking about. Quiet kids wearing two guns at a time made him uneasy. It didn't help when Pecos didn't answer.

The one called Banger explained, "It was the last big job we pulled, year before last, I think. Kid Curry set it up, so he was in charge. The kid had heard about a safe full of cash aboard the Great Northern Express pulled by old Engine Number Three. So when they stopped for water at Malta, Montana, we clumb aboard betwixt the cars, waited till we was out of town—where the Tall Texan's sweetheart, Laura Bullion, was holding the horses—and stopped the train slick as a whistle. Me and Butch blowed the safe right, for a change. Butch is inclined to use too much nitro on his own. Anyways, we got close to fifty thousand in cash and cashier's checks without hurting a hair on anyone's head."

Will chimed in, "They split up. That's when things went to hell in a hack. The Tall Texan and Laura got picked up in Saint Lou, trying to cash one of them checks with the wrong signature. Tex was always better at shooting than forgery. Meanwhile Kid Curry, seeing he was in Montana anyway, took a solo detour to the Winters spread to gun old Jim Winters for personal reasons. Jim was sort of popular in them parts, so Kid Curry lit out for his hometown in Missouri."

"It didn't work," Banger said. "Deaf Charlie Hanks tried to cash another stolen check in Tennessee and got kilt in the resultant confusion. That alerted the Pinkertons to look east for at least some of the gang, and hell, they knew where Kid Curry hailed from."

Will nodded. "He made out better than old Deaf Charlie, though. Killed two Missouri lawmen and came back out here to get things organized again." He shot a thoughtful look at Banger and added, "Some organization. After all that planning, we wasn't able to open the safe on that last train, and my share of the passenger money comes to about what I could make herding cows a month, a lot less nervous."

Stringer got his smoke going, with some difficulty, and since he didn't want them fighting among themselves until he'd had time to plan what he might do, he soothed, "Well, at least nobody got hurt, and thanks to that rain last night, I don't see how the law can trail you all the way back to the Hole in the Wall."

The two outlaws facing him looked blank. "Who told you we was headed up to them old haunts?" Banger asked.

Stringer shrugged. "Kid Curry, of course," he answered truthfully enough. "Didn't he tell *you* about Brown's Hole, up in the headwaters of the Green?"

Nobody answered for a moment. Then Banger said, "That tears it. I might have known when Butch and Sundance didn't show up for this job that they figured Curry'd gone loco, total!"

"Let's be fair," Will said to him. "You know some say Butch and Sundance left the country, or at least they went back east a spell. It wasn't Kid Curry's fault that they put that sneaky new safe aboard that train. Save for that, everything went slick as usual."

Banger shook his head. "The hell you say. He told us he had a hideout we'd be safe in, after. Yet he told this newspaper gent we was headed back to the Hole in the Wall!"

"He might have had some other hole in another wall in mind," Will suggested. "Where in the U.S. Constitution do it say we have to leave a permanent address on file with the law?"

Banger stared morosely at the sick man under the blanket between them. "Slim's done for," he said. "We're just asking to get caught if we stay here much longer."

Will said, "Kid Curry may not take it kindly if we leave him here like this."

"That's what I just said," Banger replied. "Without Butch here to keep Kid Curry calm and laughing, he's just plain mean. I never did think he was all that smart. I don't know where the hell he thinks he's heading now, and I for one don't care. I just risked my freedom for next to nothing, and I don't mean to lose it entire by following a lunatic one mile farther."

He got to his feet. "I'm going to double back and see if I can catch a train to Denver or someplace as sensible. Are you coming with me or do you still buy that yarn about the tooth fairy, Will?"

His sidekick hesitated, then rose with a nod and turned to the man up the slope. "He's right, Pecos. Kid Curry's lost his touch. This reporter gent can look after Slim, and I for one will be proud to protect your sweet ass from the law."

Pecos replied in a grim but surprisingly sissy voice for a two-gun man of any age. "You mention my sweet ass one more time and I'll kill you," he said. "I got kin riding with the Wild Bunch, and we all agreed Kid Curry was the leader on this raid. You all can bugger out if you've a mind to. Men with no balls ain't no use to the outfit anyways."

Will laughed, then made the mistake of jeering, "Take down them britches and spread your sweet cheeks and I'll just show you who's got balls or not."

So Pecos killed him.

Banger had to have been as surprised as Stringer by such a lightning draw. But both he and Stringer came unstuck by the time Will flopped all the way down to the grass, lifeless as a wet dishrag. Then Banger was going for his own gun, and Stringer, having nothing better to aim, had pulled up a clump of grass by the muddy roots and thrown it at him.

It might have thrown Banger's timing off. It might not have really mattered, for Pecos caught him over the right eyebrow with a second round, and he fell dead and literally brainless with his gun still gripped in its holster.

Pecos was sitting and Stringer was on one knee on the

grassy slope, the sounds of gunfire still echoing from the hills all around, when Pecos began to cry, sobbing. "Damn it, I never asked to be birthed a girl, you know."

Stringer did know now. It was surprising how disgusting a young gent looked with such a pouty baby face when one considered how nice the same cameo features fit even a he-dressed she. But Pecos still had that smoking gun out. So Stringer chose his words carefully as he told her, "You're fast enough for a gunslick of any persuasion, Miss Pecos. If they already knew you was a gal, it serves 'em right for talking so dirty in front of you."

Pecos sniffed. "I'm still sorry I lost my temper," she said. "Old Will had that coming and Banger should have stayed out of it. But what vexes me now is that any lawman within miles could have heard them shots. We got to get Slim mounted and consider some serious riding, hear?"

Stringer moved over to the sick lunger and felt Slim's head. It was too feverish to worry anyone about him being alive. But Stringer could feel Slim's pulse anyway, in the throbbing veins of his dry hot temples. "If you want him dead, just put a third bullet in him," he told Pecos. "It won't discomfort him as much as hauling him around might, but the results will likely be the same."

Then he tried, "You ride on if you're afraid they're closing in on us, Pecos. They won't arrest me, and I'll be proud to stay here with old Slim."

It didn't work. "That well may be," she said. "But they'll hang Slim for sure as soon as he's up to it. Do you know that when they hanged Black Jack Ketchum, it tore his head clean off?"

Stringer grimaced. "Well, things like that can happen if they don't figure the drop just right. But they might not hang old Slim here. Didn't they just put the Tall Texan and his moll in prison when they were caught in Saint Lou?"

Pecos shook her head. "Tex Kilpatrick never kilt nobody, and all poor old Laura was good at was screwing. Slim, there, is wanted for more than one killing. I don't mean to leave him here for the law whilst I still have any bullets left."

That seemed to remind her she ought to reload, and Stringer had already noticed all the .44-40 rounds in her cartridge belt. So as she fed her six-gun, Stringer rose, saying, "You might have a time explaining more recent shootings when and if a posse gets here. So why don't I just drag these old boys into the mine and let the rats worry about 'em?"

That didn't work either. As he moved over to the bodies down the slope a few yards, Pecos said, "Unbuckle their gun rigs, slow, where I can still see you doing it. I know you gave your parole, but I ain't as stupid as I might look to you."

Stringer smiled sheepishly and then, since the lady still had a big gun in her little fist, he did as he was told. Then he got a grip on Banger's boot heels and hauled him off the grass and across the mud to the mine adit. The rock floor inside was almost as slick. So it was easy enough to leave the body about where he'd been forced to spend last night.

It wasn't until he'd done the same for old Will, dragging him a few yards deeper into the mine, that Stringer noticed something odd. Dragging the two bodies hadn't sweated him enough to matter, but he still felt air on his cheek, blowing the wrong way. He sniffed and noticed the mysterious breeze didn't smell stinky enough for expanding mine gas, and it was a hard-rock mine to begin with. So what was left?

Stringer hunkered down to go through the pockets of the two dead men. He'd been hoping for a derringer. He wound up with just over a hundred dollars in paper and change, along with one of those fancy new cigar lighters that ran on benzine. He flicked it on. You could sure see a lot better in a mine with a cigar lighter. The big flickering flame said he was right about that air current too. He moved gingerly but deeper into the abandoned mine. Kid Curry had warned him the timbers back this way were rotten. But the ones he'd passed so far looked solid enough. So did the granite roof, until he came to a caved-in stretch where said roof had come down to almost block the passage. But almost wasn't entire. The lighter was throwing orange rays. That rock pile was sort of blue-lit in places. He flicked the lighter off. He could still see almost as well, for daylight was coming down through the big hole in the roof.

Stringer stared morosely up at the little circle of blue sky high above him. While he saw at a glance he could have done a Santa Claus in reverse the night before, if only he'd known, it was a mite late to consider now. "Shit," he muttered. "This is a fine time to tell me."

The recent cave-in Kid Curry couldn't have known about was little use to anyone now that Curry and all those horses in and about the front entrance were long gone. He stared up at the teasing patch of sky some more as he weighed his chances at the moment. They weren't half so good in broad-ass day with an armed and dangerous woman on the far slope of the little valley, likely gazing more or less this way. Even if he could pop out of the far slope like a gopher and she missed him at that range, he'd still be too close to her for comfort, and she had just warned him not to take her for a fool. There was no way to get away from Pecos with neither a mount nor a gun to call his own. He considered every way he'd ever heard of to avoid the company of an armed and mounted enemy in country one might not know half as well as the other side.

Then he finished rolling the dumb smoke he'd started without thinking, lit it with his fancy new cigar lighter, and headed back to see if he could make the pretty little thing a friend instead of an enemy.

By the time he got back to Slim and Pecos, it was already warming up considerable. Pecos had opened her jacket and tossed the big black hat aside on the grass. This gave the effect of someone sticking the head of a Gibson Girl atop the body of a shabby two-gun saddle tramp—although with the jacket open, she bulged more female under her hickory shirt.

He didn't sit down with them right off. "When and if we ever ride on," he said, "those ponies will carry us farther if they feel less abused. With your permission, I mean to unsaddle and graze 'em out here in the sunlight. It wouldn't hurt their saddle blankets all that much, either, if I spread 'em on the grass to dry."

She frowned up at him. "We'll never get all five rounded up and resaddled soon enough to matter if a posse comes busting over yonder ridge, damn it."

He nodded but insisted, "Life is a gamble, and the house has to win in the end. Meanwhile it pays to study the odds. The law may or may not be on our trail. Those ponies figure to get sick, sure, if we don't start treating them better. You can see Slim, here, won't be riding anywhere for a spell. But I've been studying on your own situation. If we see anyone coming over that ridge to the south, your best bet is the mine adit. You can make it easy before anyone can ride within rifle range, and once they're down here, they'll hesitate pretty good before they'll risk going head first into a hole in the ground after even a lady with two guns."

She smiled bitterly. "Hell, why should they? Anyone

can see that once they had me denned like a fox in that one-way burrow, they'd just have to wait me out until I gave up or shot my fool self."

"That's what they'd do, all right," he said. "They'd just hunker down around the adit and cuss down the shaft at you. But, you see, there's another way out. You'd have to wait until dark, of course, but once the slopes all around got more star-lit, you'd be in fine shape to crawl up and out a sort of rabbit hole two thirds of the way up yonder. You can't see it from here, even by broad day. So why would anyone in the posse be expecting you to pop out of it?"

She stared up at him thoughtfully for a long silent moment before she said, "I think you're just funning me. How come we was able to hold you prisoner overnight in that mine if, all the time, you knew of a way to get out?"

He shrugged. "I gave my parole," he lied. "Even if I hadn't, I'm a newspaper man. I'd be a fool to let a news feature like this get away from me. Nobody outside your gang has ever given the true facts to any outsider, and I've already discovered the outside world has a lot of misconceptions about the Wild Bunch. Can I see to those ponies now?"

She rose gracefully to her feet. "Leave 'em be. None of 'em suffer from TB like Slim, and they was watered and oated only an hour or so ago. I want you to show me that rabbit hole, and for your sake, it had better be there."

He said he never argued with a lady with two guns, and led her along the contour above the level of the mine yard and adit to save needless mountain climbing. When they'd worked their way around to more or less above the tunnel below, he waved upslope and said, "Hold your fire if I have to zigzag some. I've only seen the bottom of the hole so far, and this ungrazed elk grass may make the finding of the top a chore."

He was righter than he'd wanted to be. They'd worked their way farther up the slope than he'd figured on, and Pecos was starting to cuss as well as pant in the thin mountain air when he suddenly spotted a patch ahead where no grass tops seemed to be growing. "Watch your step," he cautioned her. "It's a hell of a ways down, almost straight." Then he dropped to his hands and knees to crawl up the last few yards. Pecos did the same. So they were soon on their mutual knees, hip to hip, staring down what looked more like a bottomless garbage pit than anything else that might belong up here in the middle of nowhere.

Pecos laughed like a little kid who'd just noticed someone bringing her birthday cake from the kitchen. "I thought you was funning. But hold on. How does one find the bottom end in that maze below?"

"You just keep moving back until you see daylight, of course," he said. "There's no maze. The old-timers just followed one vein under this slope until it pinched out. But if you need exact directions, I left Banger and Will just this side of a big old rock pile. The rock pile's directly under us right now. As you can see, it's a considerable climb. But the walls are lumpy enough to offer plenty of hand and foot holes."

She looked around. "This tall grass is made for crawling too."

"I'd still wait for dark before I tried that," he said. "Grass tops move, and you know how nosy some posse riders can get, even when they can't see what's making things move when the wind's not blowing."

Pecos moved back from the hole and rolled on one hip and elbow as she stared down the slope. From up there the tethered ponies looked like mice and poor old Slim looked like he was sandwiched between two bitty postage stamps. She sighed. "I wish I'd thought to bring a picnic basket up here with us. Wouldn't this be a fine place for a picnic, MacKail?"

He found a comfortable position beside her. "My friends call me Stuart. Did they really sprinkle you as Pecos?"

She sighed. "Not hardly. My real name's Opal. Opal Place."

Stringer shot her a curious look. "Do tell? I hear the Sundance Kid keeps company with a runaway schoolmarm called Etta Place. Might you and she be kin, Opal?"

Pecos chuckled fondly. "Etta's my first cousin, and we're the only kin either of us have, now that nobody else in the family will have anything to do with us. You got the part about her being a runaway right. But I don't recall her ever teaching any school. Old Etta was working for Madam Fannie Porter in Fort Worth, with Annie Rogers, when Sundance and Kid Curry decided it made more sense to keep a private whore than to risk riding into town every time they wanted some slap-and-tickle. So they got Etta and Annie to run off with 'em."

Stringer smiled thinly. "The schoolmarm version is more likely to go down in history. I didn't know the Wild Bunch worked that far south. Of course, if anyone else knew just where they might show up, they might not spend so much time at large. Do they call you Pecos because you, ah, worked in Texas one time, Opal?"

She shook her head. "Not as a whore, if that's what you mean. Like Etta, I had to get away from our more sedate kin before they druv me crazy with all that praying about hellfire and damnation. But I wasn't half as wild as her. I got away from home young by eloping with a cow thief. We had us a nice little spread on the Pecos for a spell afore things started to go wrong."

"What went wrong? Did the law catch up with your man?" he asked.

"No. He caught up with a bottle. You'd have to be a woman to understand, I reckon. I've found that all I have to tell most women, even real schoolmarms, is that I made the mistake of marrying up with a drinking man, and then I don't have to tell 'em another word."

Stringer nodded soberly. "I get the picture. But how did you wind up riding with the Wild Bunch, in pants, after you left your husband?"

"I couldn't go home," she said. "I was still wearing skirts a lot more when I took up with Grat Winslow. You met him last night when we stopped your train. He was the one who rid upstream when the rest of us rid down."

Stringer cocked an eyebrow at her. "You must not have been too fond of him."

"Oh, Grat was all right, if you don't mind strong and stupid," she said. "I can't even rightly say it was dumb of him to desert like that. You see, it was my notion, not his, to join Kid Curry and the others in these parts when Curry sent out word he was putting the Wild Bunch back together for a grand train robbery. You saw what a poor haul we made in the end. I was tempted to ride off with Grat last night. But like I told them others, I got kin riding with the outfit. I've been trying to hook up with my cousin Etta again. Once I do, I might be able to talk her into leaving with me so's we could go into some better-paying business together. I know lots of things now about running brands and forgin' bills of sale."

Stringer grinned. "I'm sure you do. But everyone keeps telling me that Butch Cassidy, Sundance, and your cousin Etta have left the country, Opal."

She shrugged. "The same story was going around when Butch and Kid Curry stopped old Engine Number Three. It was likely Etta who talked Sundance out of going along that time. She's a smart old gal. She made it almost through high school afore she run off to be a whore. She likely guessed correct about the way that last big job would turn out. I know they say she and Sundance have a sheep spread in the Argentine right now. On the other hand, a friend of mine spotted her in Cheyenne just a few months back, and folk was getting letters from South America from all three of them at the very time Butch and Kid Curry was stopping that old express train in Montana. So I'm hoping we'll meet up with Etta and the others up the trail, as the old gang gets back together again, see?"

Stringer suspected he was starting to see more about the way the Wild Bunch really functioned than he was supposed to. So he didn't mention the fact that Pecos was probably right about her cousin being in the Cheyenne area at the moment. He hoped like hell she'd stay there, for if his suspicions about a certain mighty pretty gal he'd spent a night with just north of Cheyenne were at all correct, he sure didn't want to meet up with her again in the company of the Sundance Kid—with or without a gun of his own handy.

But he felt it was safe to ask just what Cousin Etta might look like, so risked adding, "I hear tell she sometimes tries to pass herself off as a Cherokee breed."

"That's even wilder than schoolmarm," Pecos replied. "But I reckon she could if she had to. Both of us are sort of dark Welsh-blooded. But don't mention such matters to Kid Curry when we catch up with him and the others. He gunned a man in Billings once for asking if him and his brothers might have Indian blood."

"I'll try to remember that," Stringer said. "But is Kid Curry a breed? I can't say he looks like one."

She grimaced. "Some say he's part Cherokee. Sundance

told Etta, one night when he was drunk, that all the Logan boys was part colored. You're right about it not showing. But Johnny Logan did have sort of kinky hair, and some say curious remarks about that led to his shootout with Jim Winters a spell back."

"Thanks for warning me they're so sensitive," Stringer said. "Kid Curry promised to introduce me to both his brothers when we join the main bunch, wherever."

Pecos shot him a curious look. "Now why would he say a thing like that, Stuart? Didn't you know both his brothers is dead?"

He blinked in surprise. "Not until you just now mentioned it. Wouldn't *he* have heard about such sad news by now?"

"He must have been greening you," she said. "Johnny was blown half in two by Jim Winters's shotgun in Montana, back in '96. Old Lonny Logan bled to death in the snow when the law caught up with him in the winter of '99. You say Kid Curry offered to introduce you to 'em, personal?"

Stringer nodded. "Let's hope you're right and that he was just funning. I don't see how he could expect me to publish nice things about him if he means to send me where his brothers went. I'm not sure I deserve to go the same place, in any case."

She was staring at him sort of wide-eyed and worried. "Etta always said Kid Curry was too crazy for her Sundance to hang out with. Butch lit out and never showed up no more after Curry rid so far out of the way to gun Jim Winters and them two lawmen just as the law was losing interest in that last big train robbery. Do you reckon them two gents I had to shoot could have been right about Curry losing his grip on the real old world the rest of us is stuck in?"

Stringer moved closer and tried to guess the odds on putting a comforting arm around her versus those of drawing back a ways. He knew women well enough to sense she might be less worried about him right now than her chosen leader. He kept his voice soothing as he told her, "The kid no doubt has more on his mind to vex him than you and me. The law's not after me at all, and they may not be interested in you either, if you kept better company."

"What about Slim?" she asked.

"I agree it would be mean to leave him behind. But where does it say we have to ride after the others with him? There's lots of places to ride in this real old world, you know. It was Kid Curry who rode off on us when a pal got sick. You just said yourself that your kinswoman, Etta, may not want Sundance to play with him no more. I can see how a man who doesn't seem to know where he's going, and offers to introduce you to dead folk when you get there, could make any lady with a lick of sense consider thinking for her own self."

She sat up and hugged her knees, thinking hard indeed. Since she hadn't flinched the last time he'd edged closer, Stringer tried another few inches, and she didn't seem to notice. He was close enough now for a lightning grab at the .44-40 riding her hip on his side. But then what? She still had another gun on her far hip.

Stringer knew the answer. He'd always wondered if false-hearted women buttering up a man to take advantage felt as shitty as they ought to. He knew it made *him* feel a little shitty, lying to many a sweet young thing when all he was after was sweet romance. This one was less likely to call a man a brute after he'd had his way with her. He'd already seen her kill two men, and he knew any man who tried to argue with her after grabbing one of her guns was just asking for sudden death from the other. But did he really want to escape that badly?

His objective mind told him he did. He'd already learned a lot more than any outsiders were supposed to know about the Wild Bunch, and the contract he'd signed with the *San Francisco Sun* hadn't been a suicide pact. Kid Curry was unstable, and even if he remembered the deal they'd made, some of the others had already shown they didn't care for outsiders tagging along. He knew he'd never get a better chance to get out of this mess. But the part of his brain that dealt with his emotions still thought that murdering a pretty girl, even a murderous one, was just plain wrong.

He was still arguing inside his skull about it when a shadow fell across them. Pecos had drew away from him and drawn her gun before Stringer could even look up. Then they both saw it was Slim. The lunger looked like a walking corpse.

Pecos put her gun away again as Stringer said, "Howdy. You sure look awful, Slim. How do you feel?"

"Tolerable," Slim said. "I just hawked up a mess of bloody oysters and then I noticed nobody was around. What are you two doing way the hell up here?"

"Nothing, thanks to you," Pecos said. "Do you feel in shape to ride on, Slim?"

The skinny, pallid owlhoot patted the six-gun against his thigh. "This makes me strong as I need to be, I reckon. Where did all the others go?"

Pecos rolled to her feet. "I'll have us there afore supper-time. I rid with Grat and the kid all over these parts as they scouted the country whilst planning that robbery. They'll be holed up in a canyon we found. Or maybe I ought to say Kid Curry found it. He'd been working as a cowhand hereabouts for months before he called the rest of us in from near and far."

As the three of them headed back down the slope, Stringer could see that Pecos was upset about something, and decided it was best to let her species work such mysterious moods out on their own. They were almost down to the ponies before she asked him, "If Slim hadn't woke up just now, was you fixing to kiss me or go for my gun, MacKail?"

He laughed like hell and assured her neither thought had even crossed his mind. For some reason that made her cuss all men in a most unladylike way.

CHAPTER
FOUR

They rode well into the afternoon before Slim started coughing bad again. Pecos called a halt where the invisible trail she seemed to be following led through a jumble of house-sized boulders and wind-twisted juniper. Slim said he was all right, but Pecos told him to get down anyway, adding, "It's time for you two men to change to the spare mounts Banger and Will were kind enough to leave us. I watch my figure better, so my old paint ought to last through the day."

She pointed at a sand-filled sunlit hollow among the rocks. "Spread Will's tarp yonder," she told Stringer, "and Slim can repose a spell whilst we water and rest the ponies."

Slim was still arguing about it, but since it made sense to Stringer, he did as he was told. By the time he'd built a sort of nest for Slim in the warm, dry den, Pecos had poured canteen water in the nose bags that came with every saddle. The brutes had been allowed to crop grass every time they'd stopped for a few minutes' rest out of each hour. Water was always the real problem.

Once they had Slim bedded down with his own canteen and some opium pills he took for his lungs, Pecos scrambled up the rocks like a squirrel, albeit Stringer noticed her jean-covered rump was prettier. When Slim asked Stringer where the fool gal might be going, Stringer said, "For a lookout, most likely. Don't take enough of that opium to knock yourself out entire. I'll follow her topside and see what she's up to."

He did. There were plenty of toeholds in the rounded elephant-gray granite. When he got to the top, he found Pecos stretched out prone in yet another sandy hollow, peering anxiously over the south rim. She'd put her ugly hat back on. But it was still hard to see how he'd ever mistaken her for a young boy, now that he knew what her baggy jacket and sun-faded jeans really covered. As he moved to lie down beside her, she rolled on one side and drew on him. "Don't creep up on a gal like that," she said.

He reclined facing her. "Sorry, pard. I thought I made plenty of noise scraping up all those rocks just now. See anything back yonder?"

She shook her head and tossed her hat aside again. "Not even a buzzard, thanks to the way you got rid of Banger and Will. I think we've lost any posse out after us. I sure hope so. What do you think?"

He peered out across treetops and rocky ridges as far as the eye could see, and from up here one could see a hell of a ways. "I can't even tell where I am right now," he said. "I'm lost as hell. On the other hand, some of the local cowhands who failed to join Kid Curry might well have signed on with the posse. Did your man Grat know about that canyon you mentioned, Pecos?"

"Sure he did, but he ain't my man no more, and you can call me Opal some more if you've a mind to. I hadn't been getting along so well with Grat *before* he deserted us."

Stringer got rid of his own hat and rose to his knees for a better look south as he said, "If they didn't follow the rest of us down that whitewater creek last night, they might have followed old Grat up it. You say he's been working in these parts as a cowhand, Opal?"

"Sure," she said. "It's dumb to tell folk you're a train robber when you ain't robbing trains. What difference does it make, now that Grat's long gone?"

"It could make a lot of difference if Grat meets up with any posse and fails to convince them he's just a good old boy who belongs in these parts. Do you figure he's smart enough to lie instead of run for it when he bumps noses with the law?"

She stared soberly up at him. "Land's sakes if you ain't sly! I don't know if Grat's that smart, but if he is, he just might get away with it."

He lay back down beside her. "You'd know him better. He might even be slick enough to join any posse he runs into. I don't suppose he'd lead them to that mysterious canyon for the reward on at least Kid Curry, right?"

She gasped. "Oh, Lord, there is a lot of paper out on the kid, Slim, and half the others, now that I study on it. I told you me and Grat hadn't been getting on so well of late, and if Grat felt all that devoted to Kid Curry, he'd have never rid off on us like that!"

Stringer moved a little closer on the soft sand, saying, "All in all, I'd say that canyon you've been leading us to all day might not be the best place to keep heading for."

"You're wrong," she said. "We still got to warn our pards."

He was glad she seemed to be including him in her list

of pards now. As he placed a casual hand on hers, he said, "If the law doesn't find out about the place from Grat or anyone else, the gang doesn't need to be warned. If the law *has* found out about it, they would have hours ago. If Grat didn't manage to ride through 'em, we could be riding into a trap. Can't you see it's too late to help them if they need help, and no sense going on if they don't?"

She put her free hand on her topside gun as she sighed. "I can see how you could be trying to lead me down the primrose path to perdition too. You must be able to tell I think you're pretty as well as sweet-talking. But I've been lied to by many a man in my life, and this is a mighty serious game we're playing."

She didn't draw. So he didn't let go her other hand as he told her, "Banger and Will would no doubt agree. But I'm not out to trick you, Opal. It's the sure path to perdition I'm trying to lead you and even old Slim away from."

"That's easier to say than prove," she said.

"If you'll kindly refrain from drawing that gun, I may be able to convince you of my sincere good will, honey."

"I ain't sure I want you to call me honey just yet," she replied. "But what did you have in mind?"

He reached under his jacket with his own free hand. "I'm about to draw a gun," he said. "Not at you. To show you. Keep it in mind that I'm keeping my trigger finger out of the trigger guard and know better than to point any gun at anyone I don't mean to shoot."

Then he showed her the nickel-plated Harrington & Richardson .32 he'd found in Will's bedroll a few minutes before. But when she asked him, soberly, where he'd gotten it and how long he'd had it he saw no reason to refrain from looking her right in the eye and saying, "I learned to pick pockets covering another outlaw gang one time. The point is, I've had all day and a lot of chances to do you or Slim dirty if that was my intent."

She looked so relieved that he saw no need to elaborate on why the last owner had packed it away like that. It was a sort of pretty little whore pistol, and if ever a gunsmith got around to fixing the busted mainspring, it might even shoot again.

Opal could see it was loaded, and he quickly put it away before she could ask him to fire it at anything. "I reckon it's all right for you to call me honey, then," she said. "But you sure are a sneaky rascal."

They both laughed. Then he noticed how warm and languid her hazel eyes were getting and that she'd let go her gun grips. So it seemed only natural to reel her in and kiss her.

She kissed back in a way that made him believe she hadn't been getting along with her deserting lover of late. But when he started to unbutton her hickory shirt with his free hand, she protested, mildly, "Hold on. What if old Slim decides to come up here?"

"The hell with him," Stringer growled. "Let him get his own gal."

"Oh, well," she sighed. "We're going to look just as ridiculous doing it with our duds on as off, I reckon."

But he still found things complicated, once he had her gun rig set aside and her shirt unbuttoned down the front. For the current dictates of Edwardian fashion had things all bass-ackwards. Even the sassy young modern gals old Charles Dana Gibson drew wore skirts and rode sidesaddle in the same. It was widely held that only a downright harlot would be seen riding astride or wearing pants at any time. Yet anyone with a lick of common sense could see the longest skirt had pants beat hollow when it came to getting *at* a woman.

That got him to reconsidering a family tradition, and when he chuckled, Opal asked if he was laughing at her tits. He kissed the nipple of the one he had a grip on and assured her he liked her cupcakes just fine. That part, at least, was true. He'd thought she was just naturally dark until he'd gotten her creamy chest exposed to the afternoon sunlight. Her young body was firm and athletic, even where the sun and wind couldn't get at it, and her breasts, while a mite small, were firm and formed delightfully. When she still wanted to know what was so funny if it wasn't her exposed chest, he told her, "I was just recalling what my Uncle Donald told me as a shaver about the old country our clan came from. Back there we ran about in kilts and enjoyed a rep for raping cows and stealing women. I used to think a man looked sissy in checkerboard kilts. But I can see certain advantages to 'em right now."

"You'll never get these jeans of mine down unless I help," she said. "Get rid of your own, and that jacket too. The gun in your inside pocket hurts my ribs, not even bouncing."

So they parted company just long enough to shuck at least those parts of their costume that got in the way. She somehow looked even more naked with her open shirt and jacket on as he rolled aboard her in just his shirt, with his own jeans down around his ankles. Then he'd entered her and they both went deliciously crazy for a spell. But after he'd ejaculated in her, his brain began to function better, and while he wasn't rude enough to take it out of a lady while she was still moaning and groaning, he did find himself staring thoughtfully at the two guns she'd tossed to the sand, almost within reach.

Opal seemed to be taking his somewhat distracted movements as consideration. "Oh, Jesus," she crooned, "this sure feels lovely, and I fear you're going to have a hard time getting rid of me, Stuart MacKail!"

That might have cooled him off like a bucket of spring-water if she hadn't been so pretty and been gripping him so tightly with her warm internal contractions. He found himself moving faster with her, even as the logical parts of his mind weighed how much he liked her against how badly he wanted to get away.

He knew how much he'd hurt her if he got the drop on her now. It would be just as kind, and no doubt safer, to just haul off and knock her out as she lay spread eagle and exposed to a sucker punch to her pretty little chin. But that still left Slim, down below, and Slim had been left in charge of the two gun belts old Banger and Will had no further use for.

He knew he might be able to knock Opal out and get her two guns without really harming her all that much. The only way in hell he'd get by Slim, if Slim was even half awake, would be to slide down the rocks shooting. Neither Opal nor Slim were given to meditation. Both were too dangerous to mess lightly with. As he went on making love to Opal, he wondered, as he'd sometimes wondered before, whether he might be too decent for his own good or an outright coward.

He knew real gunslicks never hesitated. That was what made them gunslicks. He who hesitated in a stand-up confrontation between armed men—or women, come to think of it—was lost. A lot of good men had died in those split seconds it takes for a sensible cuss to decide whether this was for real or whether one could still talk one's way out of it. He had come close to dying that way, more than once, and every time he'd managed to come out alive, he'd promised himself that never again would he think twice if another armed man even looked at him ugly. Yet here he was, doing it again, and what in thunder was he waiting for?

"I like it slow like that, up to a point," Opal said. "But now I'm getting to that point again and . . . I know. Let me get on top."

He did. He could think even better on his back with her doing all the work. But damn, she sure looked pretty as she crouched over him like that, moving her bare bottom so sassy. As if she'd read his mind, she smiled down at him and said, "I don't care what they say, I like it like this in the daytime, when we can see what we're doing to each other. Do you like it this dirty, too, honey?"

"It's not dirty," he said. "I've got my jacket under my bare rump and the sand up here was clean to begin with."

She started moving faster, panting. "Oh, yesss! It does feel clean and natural, like we was Adam and Eve afore they was taught shame by the Lord. I've never understood that part of the Good Book. I mean, don't it seem silly they'd have felt the need to wear fig leaves right after they'd been screwing in that garden with nary another soul to peek at 'em?"

"I sometimes suspect all the rules and regulations about duds were made up by older folk," he said, "after they noticed they didn't look so fine bareass. Most gents don't get religion until they get to feeling older and mayhaps calmer, and anyone can see how an old potbellied prophet might feel more dignified wearing a toga or whatever."

Then they didn't talk about it any more for a spell, because they were too busy coming together. Opal collapsed weakly down on him, sobbing. "Oh, I just can't move no more, and I've never been any happier. Does it vex you to just lay still like this?"

"Nope," he said. "I feel happy too. Let me get my second wind and I'll be proud to get on top and show you how happy I am."

But she said, "Hold on. I have to see if I was imagining things just now. To tell the truth, it didn't seem to matter whilst I was coming."

She sat up straight. He found the view inspiring. But she wasn't looking down at him. She'd raised a hand to shield her eyes against the afternoon sun as she stared off at something off to the southwest. When he asked what she was looking at, she told him, "Riders. Along a ridge a good ten miles or more from here, thank God. They don't seem to be headed this way after all. You want to get on top now?"

He told her to hold the thought, and gently rolled her off his lap so he could sit up and see what she was talking about. He didn't see anything at first. The sun in his eyes made the ridges over that way a confusion of jagged cardboard cutouts, darker closer in and sort of misty purple farther out. Then he spotted what looked like bitty sugar ants crawling along a cardboard edge against the cloudless sky. "Yep," he muttered, "that's a posse, sure as hell. Wrong time of the year for roundup, and I can't think of anything else that would have so many gents riding in a bunch that big."

"Well, whoever they may be," she said, "they're riding the wrong way entire. I told you I know this range pretty good. There's an old Injun trail along that ridge. I wonder why they're on it."

He asked where the mysterious trail might lead.

"Utah," she replied. "Do you follow it far enough."

"There you go. If your Grat Winslow is on his way to the north-south outlaw trails that follow the trend of the Green south, it could be his sign that posse's following.

Didn't you say your lover knows the way to your real hide-out?"

It didn't work. "Don't worry about that," Opal said. "If it's Grat they're trailing, and I hope it is, he's got too good a lead on them for them to ever catch him now." She added, "I wish you'd quit calling him my lover, or my anything. I just told you that you're my only true love now."

Not knowing just how to answer that, he didn't. He was glad he might not have to coldcock her and murder Slim after all. If he couldn't talk her into hiving off from the Wild Bunch with him to somewhere more sensible, and likely feeling mighty sore at him later, he could still hope for rescue once that posse caught up with old Grat and made him talk.

Stringer didn't share her optimistic views on Grat's lead. It seemed to him that the deserter had showed more cowardly panic than common sense when he'd left them riding upstream, to the east. If he was now headed west, along a well-known route, it read that Grat had circled wide in the dark, hoping not to leave sign, and then the posse had read his sign anyway. That meant the fugitive must have hit the old Indian trail after that last heavy rain, and it hadn't stopped raining until almost dawn. Say Grat had been riding west no more than a few hours longer than Opal had been leading them north, that put him six or eight hours ahead of the posse down yonder, on a horse he'd ridden longer than most horses liked to be ridden. One couldn't tell from this distance, but if that posse wasn't traveling that fast with spare mounts, they were even dumber than old Grat. Since that hardly seemed possible, Stringer figured they'd catch up with him sometime after dark, even if Grat wasn't dumb enough to light a fire.

As the distant dotted line dropped below the skyline

once more, Opal said, "I hope we've seen the last of 'em. We'd still better push on and tell Kid Curry and the others. They might still be worried."

As they started to get dressed again, Stringer was feeling even better than the average man who'd just made love to a beautiful woman. He was a newspaper man, after all, and he could no doubt keep Kid Curry bragging and in a good mood for the next twelve hours or so. Old Sam Barca, at the features desk, would never forgive him if he missed a chance to cover the capture of the one and original Wild Bunch.

Opal rose to put her guns and hat back on. "I'd forgotten how nice it feels with no rubber," she told him. "But just the same, from now on we'd best not take chances. Here." She handed him a sealed box of Pasha condoms. "You'd best carry these for us. I fear I'm too weak-willed to stop and consider the odds when I get hot."

He put the contraceptives away without comment, somewhat assured by the fact she hadn't seen fit to open the packet since she'd no doubt asked Grat Winslow to buy them. Of course, since she'd just said she was weak-willed, it worked two ways.

They climbed back down to find Slim on his feet again. The lunger's cheeks looked as if they'd been rouged. But he seemed chipper enough. "Them pills and a little dry sweating was just what I needed," he said. "Where have you two been all this time? I was about to come looking for you."

Stringer didn't answer. He was surprised when Opal told Slim in a surprisingly casual tone, "We was screwing. MacKail, here, is my new man. Spread the word when we rejoin the others. I don't want any of the boys getting notions about me just because they don't see Grat around no more."

Slim looked more concerned than shocked. He nodded, but told her, "I'm a train robber, not a pimp. You two can tell 'em anything you want. But I hope you know you're putting an unarmed outsider in a mighty tight spot if you go bragging about him being more to your fancy than anyone else. I thought you understood that the Wild Bunch takes a sort of communal interest in gals, seeing there ain't all that many riding with us at once."

She frowned. "Pooh, I ain't a pass-about like poor old Laura Bullion was afore the Tall Texan made her his private stock. Does Kid Curry share his Annie? Does Sundance share my cousin Etta?"

"No," Slim said. "But both of them pack guns, and they've both had to defend their women with 'em on occasion."

CHAPTER
FIVE

As he finally figured out where they were going, an hour or more later, Stringer could see how the term "Hole in the Wall" might have gotten started. Pecos, as she insisted on being called again in mixed company, seemed to be leading them smack into a blank wall of sky-high rocks. Then, as they topped a rise and he could see the base of the escarpment better, he spotted the narrow entrance of a canyon, only a few feet wider than the other vertical clefts in the weather-rounded cliffs. They were approaching over slick rock. To anyone who'd picked up the little sign they'd left crossing that last stretch of soil, then lost it on the slick rock, it might well look as if they'd ridden into nowhere at all.

But as they waved and passed the sentry posted behind a boulder at the canyon mouth, and rode up the narrow cleft to where it began to open out into an amphitheater walled by sheer cliffs, it seemed harder to believe that anyone could pass within five miles and not hear all that racket.

It was easier to count horseflesh by the head than all the men and half as many women milling about Kid Curry's camp. Stringer judged their remuda as roughly a hundred-odd ponies and some mules. They'd been penned to graze at the far end of the box canyon by ropes strung on some saplings nobody had yet seen fit to cut for firewood. There were a lot more stumps than trees of any sort left standing now. The canyon could have been called well watered by the little stream that ran here and there across the rocky bottom. But the water was running thick and brown as bean soup, thanks to all the mud, wood ash, and horse shit—he hoped—the gang had been careless about. Slim had been drinking their canteen water as much as their mounts had, getting here. Both the canteens on Stringer's casually acquired saddle were now empty. He was thirsty too. But he wasn't about to refill any canteens from that stream of liquid crud.

So when Kid Curry hailed them over to where he was holding court on an ammo box near the main fire, Stringer was glad to see the kid and some of his inner circle seemed to be sharing what looked like mason jars of mineral water. As Stringer, Slim and Pecos joined them, Kid Curry handed Stringer a jar.

"I see you made it after all," he said. "What happened to Banger and Will?"

Stringer didn't feel it was his place to say. So he just took the jar and sipped from it, or started to. He'd just found out it was pure corn squeezings when Pecos said, "I had to gun 'em. They acted like they didn't have to pay no mind to a gal."

Kid Curry shrugged. "Well, I told 'em you was in

charge so don't you fret your pretty little head about it. I'll look after you, now that Grat's lit out."

"Won't your Annie Rogers have something to say about that?" Pecos asked.

Curry looked hurt as he looked off into space. He muttered, "Annie's lit out on us, too, I reckon. She was supposed to join us here, with the others. But I dunno, old Annie's been sort of brooding since I shot them last two lawmen."

In hopes of changing the subject, Stringer asked, "Where on earth did all this white lightning come from, Kid?"

That inspired Kid Curry to take the jar back and inhale an awesome gulp of the awful stuff. "Old Tom, here, brung it in with the rest of the supplies. You can never have too much liquor in snake country, you know."

A morose-looking individual seated nearby under a floppy-brimmed black hat complained, "I sure wish we could talk about the likker I packed in as much as you keep drinking it, Mr. Curry. Our deal was for cash on the barrel head, as I recall."

Kid Curry scowled at the older man. "I wish you'd listen better too," he growled. "How many times do I have to tell you we didn't get the money we expected from that last damn train?"

"I'm sorry as hell things didn't pan out better, Mr. Curry. But when you sent word about this new camp, you never said nothing about opening a line of credit. No offense, but a trader who deals with customers such as you can't afford to sell goods on time. Time has a habit of running out in your line of work."

Curry shrugged. "It's a good thing for you that you didn't water this stuff. I'm too drunk right now to stomp you right, yet not drunk enough to gun a liquor drummer, even if he is saying mean things about my spoken promises."

Arkansas, who'd been lurking in the background, moved in to put a heavy hand on the trader's shoulder. "You'd best go take a leak or something, Tom. I don't like you calling the boss a liar, neither, and I ain't drunk enough to worry about missing your fool face with my boot, hear?"

The hand on his shoulder must have weighed on old Tom's mind. He got to his feet and walked away, bitching quietly to himself. Kid Curry laughed. "Aw, Arkansas, I fear you might have hurt his feelings. Don't kill him if he wants to ride out. It's one thing to stiff an outlaw trader. It's another thing to kill him entire."

He turned to Stringer. "See how smart I am, Bathwash? Old Jesse James never would have wound up dead if he'd been smart enough to be considerate to his friends. But he went and beat the shit outten the Ford boys' uncle, and then he was dumb enough to invite 'em for supper and turn his back on the both of them."

"So I've heard," Stringer said. "You're right. It's always a good idea to be nice to folk when they let you."

Curry got sort of misty-eyed. "That's what I've always said. I wouldn't hurt a fly if it was nice to me. But for some reason folk just keep being mean to me. Why do you reckon they act that way, Bathwash?"

Stringer shrugged, gazed around at the fairly crowded camp, and offered, "You seem to have plenty of friends here."

Curry stared up at him owlishly. "Bullshit. I reckon I know who my friends are and who's just sucking around for a share of the loot. Half the men and all the women here right now, but pretty little Pecos, are just whores. They won't be staying long, now that they know how little us real men made on that last job."

He took another heroic swig from the jar, wiped his walrus moustache with his free hand, and went on, half to himself, "Good men keep getting harder to find. Sometimes I feels I'm the only one left. It seems like all the good old boys we started out with are all dead or run off somewheres. You may find this hard to buy, Bathwash, but at one time we had us over a hundred riders in the Wild Bunch, and now look what's left. Moochers and whores. Whores and moochers. They come and they go, and half the time I don't know who in the hell they are. How's a man supposed to trust folk he don't even know when half the folk he *do* know have been mean to him?"

"We're still with you, Kid," Pecos soothed. "MacKail, here, is a man anyone can trust."

If she'd been trying to help Stringer, she'd gone about it wrong. Kid Curry blinked up at them and growled, "Bullshit. He ain't one of us. He's a damned old newspaper boy who'd turn us in to the law if he could."

Pecos didn't know much about drunks for a woman who said she'd once been married to one. "No, he wouldn't," she said. "If he wasn't a man of honor, he'd be long gone by now. For it just so happens he's been packing a gun all this time."

Stringer could have kicked her. Even Slim looked a mite put out by her surprising declaration. Kid Curry started to rise, decided that might not work, and still managed to sound more sober as he asked, "Is that right, MacKail? Did you somehow manage to hang onto a gun despite our skillful friskings?"

Stringer smiled modestly. "No. I just found a bitty .32 someone must have dropped, back at that mine."

He really wanted to kick her when Pecos chimed in, "It's a six-shooting .32, though—Harrington and Richardson double action—and even though he had the edge on me and Slim, here, he never went back on his parole, see?"

Kid Curry smiled up at Stringer. "Well, I never. I reckon you ain't no sneaky backshooter after all. Why don't you find some paper, and mayhaps after supper we can get down to work on that story you mean to write about me."

Slyly, Arkansas asked, "Might we all be talking about a nickel-plated Harrison and Richardson old Will might have lost, or throwed away?"

Stringer said he had no idea who the previous owner might have been.

"I'm mighty sure it was the .32 old Will showed me," Arkansas said. "He won it in a card game a spell back."

Stringer ignored the hairs rising on the back of his neck, since right now he couldn't do anything about them unless he came up with an interesting story, fast, to account for the fact that the broken firearm in his inside pocket wouldn't fire single or double action no matter where he'd gotten it. He knew that Arkansas knew, and from the sly grin on the bully's face, he suspected Arkansas knew he knew and so forth. So why was the ugly son of a bitch holding his fire?

Arkansas didn't say. He didn't say anything as Kid Curry told Stringer, Slim, and Pecos to spread their rolls anywhere they wanted and that the grub would soon be ready if that whore he'd told to cook it knew what was good for her. Then he blinked and added, "Oh, that's right. Stringer, here, don't have no roll."

Before he could stop her, Pecos said, "That's all right. I know where he can bed down."

Stringer quickly explained, "I have two to choose from. We brought along the ponies neither Banger nor Will have any further use for."

Stringer then took the considerable risk of grabbing the girl by the arm to get her the hell away from there before she could really get him in trouble. Slim followed a short way, but said he'd see to all their ponies and left them to do so, coughing.

Since all the bedrolls anyone wanted to argue about were aboard said ponies, Stringer led Pecos to a grassy bank near the base of the cliffs. "Stay here and try to look like a boy as much as you're able," he said. "I'll rustle us up the bedrolls as soon as things settle down."

"Who are you to start giving orders around here all of a sudden?" she asked. "I don't cotton to being bossed by even a good looking man and—"

"Simmer down," he warned. "I'm not giving orders just to show I usually get on top. You talk too much, no offense, but there's still a chance Kid Curry will forget he just said dibs on you, if only you'll stay clear of him until he's too drunk to worry any woman."

She blanched and protested, "Oh, no, I don't want to screw *him,* honey!"

Stringer smiled thinly. "Neither do I. But I fear that he feels he has the right to screw both of us, should it cross his mind. So let's both stay the hell away from him for now."

He could see he'd scared her enough. So he went up the canyon to see about those bedrolls. When he got to the remuda, he saw Slim had given the job to an eager young wrangler whose mother would have no doubt had a fit if she'd known whom her boy was keeping company with when he could be safer in some opium den or ammunition plant. Stringer could only tell this because the kid had lined the familiar saddles up on the rocks outside the rope line. He told Stringer that Slim had wandered off somewhere chewing on a pocket kerchief that seemed to be covered with red polka dots.

Stringer thanked the kid for the information, and after he'd unlashed the girl's roll from her saddle, he picked the roll Banger had started out with. He didn't know for sure what might be in it. He knew he needed more than he had, so far, to work with.

He waited until he'd rejoined Pecos to explore the roll. There was nothing inside the tarp but blankets, spare socks, a bar of naptha soap, and a book of dirty pictures.

Naturally Pecos wanted to look at the dirty pictures. So he let her, leaning his back against the cliff as he fiddled with the damned fool .32. There wasn't a thing wrong with the action, save for the broken mainspring. But without said spring, the hammer just went back and stayed there when you pulled the damned trigger. It didn't lock, of course. He found he could wiggle it back and forth like the jaw of a dead parrot. He supposed that if you placed the firing pin against a round in the firing chamber, and hit the hammer hard with say a rock . . . But there had to be a better way.

He was still working on that when someone called out that the grub was ready. "I'll go fetch us some," Pecos said, and he almost told her to stay put and read dirty books while he got the coffee and grub.

Then he wondered why anyone would want to do a dumb thing like that. So he let her, saying, "Try to make it pronto, and don't tell anybody about the kind of books you read. You may know them better than me. But I'm not built so tempting. So it sort of evens out."

He'd finished fooling with the whore pistol and was reading the book, or at least the captions under the dirty pictures, when Pecos returned. She brought the franks and beans in new-looking tin plates, and the coffee was in tin cups. As she rejoined him on the tarp, Pecos said, "We got plenty of coffee and beans, honey. I reckon Kid Curry was planning on holing up here for some time."

"I never thought he was all that bright," Stringer said. "We can't be all that far from his last train robbery and— Hold on. Didn't one of those gents you shot say something about the old Green River hideout being known to the law these days?"

She nodded. "Sure, everyone knows that. I wasn't there, but I've heard others talking about how that mean old Charlie Siringo slickered even Butch Cassidy that time."

Stringer scowled down at his black coffee. "You say you, and others, have heard of Charlie Siringo? Tell me about him, honey."

"There's not much to tell," she replied. "Whilst the Wild Bunch was bigger, up yonder around Brown's Hole and Diamond Mountain, this amiable saddle tramp rid in one night, and as they fed him, he confessed he was on the run from the law because of some little misunderstanding about brands. He said his name was Carter, Charlie Carter, and Butch allowed he'd come to the right place. Like I said, I wasn't there, but it seems the skinny old cow thief hung about the Wild Bunch for a week or so. Butch even let him offer some suggestions on the best way to stop a train. The sly old dog seemed to know a lot about robbing trains. But although he agreed to help 'em stop a U.P. Flyer in a month or so, when the time came, the old-timer just wasn't there. Nobody thought much about it until they tried to stop that train and a whole damn posse jumped out of it, cussing and shooting. Our boys got away. But it was enough to make anyone study harder on who they'd been jawing with lately. I think it was Kid Curry who found out that sly old saddle tramp who called his fool self Carter was really Charlie Siringo of the Pinkertons."

She looked downright dismayed as Stringer balled up a fist and pounded his own thigh hard enough to leave bruises. When she asked what she might have said to offend him so, he hit himself some more and growled, "Oh, that lying two-faced bucket of eel puke! Not you. Not Charlie Siringo. I see it all now and I still feel dumb as hell. For I don't know whether *he* slickered me the most or *I* slickered me the most!"

She naturally asked what on earth he was talking about.

He explained, "I spoke to Charlie Siringo no more than a few weeks ago in Cheyenne and he *said* something about going out after the Wild Bunch some more. Deputy Marshal Lefors had already left Cheyenne with the same stated intention. Can't you see both of 'em must have heard Kid Curry was gathering everyone together for another big job?"

She shrugged. "So what? Neither of 'em has caught up with us so far. When Charlie Siringo led a posse of pinks to the old hideout, everyone was gone."

He nodded. "Right. And yet Kid Curry told me he'd never heard of Siringo. He also told me all of you were headed back to that hideout Charlie Siringo already knows about. Don't you get it?"

She shook her head. "Not hardly. Kid Curry keeps forgetting his brothers are dead and makes up other stuff just for fun. But he'd surely know better than to head for a place the law knew about. We spent ever so much time finding this uncharted canyon. The Kid has to know we're safer here."

Stringer sighed and muttered, "Beautiful but dumb. Think back to this morning and add it all up."

She frowned. "Well, let's see. Slim was feeling too poorly to go on, so . . ."

"Curry wasn't worried one way or the other about Slim," Stringer cut in. "He knew Banger and Will were having second thoughts about his leadership after getting so little for so much risk. He couldn't have known you and Grat Winslow hadn't been using those Pashas all that much recently. He was hoping all three of you would light out."

"What about you and Slim, then?" she asked.

"What sort of a sissy could even the Wild Bunch take me for?" he said. "Curry figured I'd have no trouble slipping away from anyone that sick."

She brightened and asked, "Oh, do you reckon he could have wanted to let you go, honey?"

"He was counting on it. He wanted me to tell the whole world the Wild Bunch was headed back to its old haunts. The lawmen searching for us right now would have thought that was mighty dumb. But since Kid Curry's done dumb things before, they might have bought it. I know *I* did, at first."

"Well, there's no harm done, lover," she said. "Now that you know Kid Curry won't really mind if you light out—"

"You can't be *that* innocent," he cut in wearily, and when he saw she seemed to be, he explained, "I was supposed to get away *before* I knew where you all were really hiding out. Now that I know about this canyon . . . Well, Kid Curry said he has plenty of booze and beans in store. I sure don't want to stay here until they're all gone, even if Curry lets me last that long!"

CHAPTER
SIX

Stringer would never know for sure whether Kid Curry had come up with the notion or whether Arkansas had simply seen a seemingly sure-fire way to add to his rep without any risk. After everyone had eaten, the sky above was still light enough to make out the bugs the bats from the canyon walls had started to chase across the gloaming lavender clifftops. Most of the bunch had gathered to take part in or at least watch the game of horseshoes someone had improvised up the canyon a piece. Not wanting to attract attention, Stringer and Pecos reclined on the tarp they were sharing at the base of the cliffs. Arkansas found them anyway.

The sardonic bully was smiling as friendly as he could manage. "Howdy, newspaper boy," he said. "I was just planning on a little target practice down the other way. We got lots of empty cans and jars to shoot at. Why don't you show us how good you are with that .32 you found?"

Stringer tried, "I'd admire that. Only I only have the five rounds I found with it."

"Hell," Arkansas said, "I can get you some more .32 rounds. Half the gals in camp favor bitty bullets for their bitty guns. What's the matter, newspaper boy? Are you afraid the noise will hurt your dainty ears?"

Stringer got wearily to his feet. "Well, I've yet to fire the piece, if it really fires. So let's not bet any money until I've had a chance to get used to the balance."

Arkansas assured Stringer they were only playing for fun. When Pecos got up, too, Arkansas said, "You'd best stay here. Target practice is for men only."

"The hell you say," Pecos replied, "I guess if you two can shoot cans, I can shoot cans, can't I?"

Arkansas shrugged. "Well, far be it from me to order Kid Curry's true love about. But you got to promise not to get in our way."

The three of them headed away from the horseshoe game and scattered bedding. The only one who seemed interested in where they might be going was the young wrangler Stringer had met before. When he asked what was up, Pecos said, "We're gonna shoot up some jars and cans." So the wrangler tagged along to watch.

The four of them got down to a slight bend in the canyon. Arkansas had already set up a row of jars and cans against the base of the cliffs. "You go first, MacKail," Arkansas said. "I want to see how good you shoot afore I risk making a fool of myself."

Stringer shrugged and drew the busted .32 from under his denim jacket. As he did so, and as he sort of expected, Arkansas roared, "Pull a gun on me, will you?" and went for his own .45.

He looked more surprised than hurt, at first, when Stringer fired the gun in his hand, three times, and put a line of button holes where Arkansas had never had any button holes before. "Aw, how did he ever do that?" Arkansas muttered, and fell in a heap at Stringer's feet.

Slim was the first to arrive who hadn't actually seen the attempted murder of Stringer. Stringer thought it best to lower the smoking muzzle politely as Slim drew, casually, and demanded to know how come old Arkansas lay dead like that.

"He started to draw on MacKail, here," Pecos said.

Slim shook his head. "You ain't exactly what I would call an objective witness, Pecos."

The young wrangler said, "Well, I don't know what you're objecting to, Slim. But I just saw what Arkansas tried to pull, and it was mighty dirty, even for him. He invited us all to shoot them jars and cans, yonder, with him. Then, when this gent took out his gun to do so, Arkansas tried to say it was personal and went for his own."

Slim stared morosely down. "I reckon I'll have to take your word on that," he murmured, "even if it sounds mighty stupid, even for Arkansas. Who but a total idjet would slap leather on any man who already had his own gun out? Anyone can see Arkansas went down with his own piece still in its fool holster."

Pecos said, "Well, he got it part ways out afore MacKail here taught him better manners. I could see he was out to collect another scalp. But you're right, it sure was dumb of him to wait that long. Mayhaps he figured it would sound more glorious if he nailed a man who had an edge on him. Who ever would have thought Arkansas was so brave?"

By this time others were arriving. Kid Curry was in the lead, walking kind of funny. He had his own gun out, but before he could shoot anybody Slim said, "It's over. Arkansas picked a fight with MacKail, here. You can see who won."

"Damn it," Kid Curry said, "I should have knowed better than to let a prisoner pack a gun, even a bitty one. You'd best hand it over, Bathwash. I got enough trouble with my real pards shooting one another up for no reason."

Stringer shrugged and handed the .32 to Slim. The lunger started to pocket it, frowned thoughtfully, and held it up to the light. "How come you put a French letter on this pistol, Stringer?" he asked. "I've heard of gents being worried about the clap, but on a gun?"

"The mainspring's busted," Stringer said. "I figured it might still fire if I twisted the rubber like that and looped it around the trigger guard and hammer spur. I'd heard you could get a gun to fire with a stout rubber band slung so. To tell the truth, I wasn't sure a Pasha would be strong enough."

Slim glanced down at the dead man between them again as he put the .32 away. "It worked better than Arkansas likely expected. I take back what I said about him being a total idjet. He was smart enough. He just run into someone a mite smarter. That's all it takes when you're playing for keeps."

"Would somebody please tell me what's going on?" Kid Curry asked. "I can see that someone tried to do someone dirty. But who did what, with what, to whoever?"

"Let's get you back to the fire afore you fall down, Kid," Slim said. "I told you it was over and all's right with the world. Arkansas tried to murder MacKail and got killed instead. I've disarmed MacKail, so he's not likely to kill nobody else this evening, see?"

"Well, I still don't like it," Kid Curry said. "He was supposed to write nice things about me for his paper, not shoot old Arkansas. We're running mighty low on real gunslicks, Slim. How am I to hold up another train if I can't get nobody but whores and runaway kids to follow me no more?"

Slim led Curry away, speaking sweet words of devotion. As Pecos led Stringer in a less dangerous direction, they both heard the young wrangler who'd helped them say, for all to hear, "I guess I know who's a grown bandit and who's still a kid around here. I may be young, but I ain't drunk, and I've yet to gun anybody dog-shit yaller."

As Stringer and Pecos walked away, they heard other ominous murmurs. The young wrangler was telling everyone who'd listen about the dirty trick Arkansas had tried. Nobody seemed interested in doing anything about his body. But the evening was still young, and they had a right to be excited about the first dead man at least some of them had ever seen.

As they got back to their own bedding and stretched out in the gathering darkness, Stringer observed, "If Kid Curry's not careful, he's likely to have a power struggle on his hands. Boys who like to take orders seldom run off with owlhoot gangs. So a leader has to sound convincing as hell, and Kid Curry just messed up that last train robbery pretty good."

"I wasn't so worried about the money," Pecos said. "I was hoping to meet up with Cousin Etta here when Kid Curry sent word the Wild Bunch was gathering again in full strength. Do you reckon Etta could have really lit out to South America with Sundance, like they say?"

Stringer shrugged. "Wherever she, Sundance, and Butch Cassidy may be tonight, they sure don't seem to be here. I'm starting to see why. Kid Curry is hardly the leader I'd choose if I ever decided on a life of crime."

"He's not so bad when he's sober," she said. "You got to admit he got us away clean, and almost slickered you whilst he was about it."

Stringer shrugged and lay back. "I reckon we all have our stupid moments. Leave my fly alone, honey. It's not dark enough for that yet."

She giggled. "I just wanted to see if you still liked me. I hope it gets dark soon. There's a position on page sixty-nine in that book that I've yet to try, and I thought I knew all of 'em by now."

He chuckled. "I know the one you mean. It won't work."

She asked how he knew, and he said, "Like most men, including the artist who drew those naughty pictures, I've got an imagination I just can't twist my torso into. Take my word for it. Even if we could get into such a wild position, it would be uncomfortable as hell."

She might have insisted on trying it anyway, later. They would never know. For just as it was getting dark enough to make out the first stars up yonder, one of the other camp followers came over to tell Pecos she was wanted at Kid Curry's fire.

Pecos got up to follow the other gal, assuring Stringer she'd be right back. He doubted that. It made him a mite angry. But she'd chosen this sort of existence, there was nothing he could do about it, and as long as he was alone for the moment in such tricky light, it would be as good a time as any to find out if he could climb the canyon walls.

He decided he might just be able to, after he'd tried here and there along the vertical but rugged cliff face. But taking such a chance, just to get to the top, made no sense unless he had somewhere to go.

Even with a full night's lead, afoot, his chances of beating the riders a no doubt pissed-off Kid Curry was likely to send after him back to civilization were slim. For one thing, he wasn't sure where civilization might be from here. They'd done some serious riding since they'd left those railroad tracks. He was sure he could make it back in time, of course. But how much time would an unarmed man on foot be given by the Wild Bunch?

He tried to tell himself they might not follow him all the way. But just how far was moot. Once Kid Curry saw he was gone, the gang would have but two choices. They could track him down and kill him before he could tell anyone else about this canyon, or they could find another hideout, fast.

Pecos, or Opal, had told him they'd had a hell of time finding this one. So, yeah, they'd try like hell to catch him, even at some risk. They'd have to. Anything else would be even riskier for them. Once he made his break, he was committed for good. All that was left to decide was whether he wanted to make a run for it on foot and unarmed, or stay here in the same grim condition until Kid Curry made up his unstable mind. Drunk or sober, sooner or later it had to occur to Kid Curry that there was just no way to let a reporter who'd interviewed you ride out of your last hideout alive. And what the hell, he had all the news about Kid Curry that was fit to print anyway.

Stringer decided to wait until later, when everyone but the guards posted near the canyon mouth would likely be drunk or at least asleep. He smoked one cigarette and was building another when Pecos rejoined him, sobbing, and flopped down beside him. "Call me Opal and get me out of this fix, honey. Kid Curry was too drunk to go all the way with me just now. But sooner or later he has to be able to get it up, and he needs a bath just awesome."

Stringer took her in his arms to comfort her, saying, "Well, if you could get us some ponies, and if you know the night guards well enough—"

"It won't work," she said, "Kid Curry must have wondered why I wouldn't call him honey lamb just now. So before he fell down entire for the night, he told everyone within earshot that I was his one true love and that he'd skin anyone who trifled with my virtue, or let me go off after Grat."

Stringer hesitated before he told her, "No matter who you want to go after, you'd best make certain in your mind that you really mean it. I noticed this afternoon that you climb rocks pretty good, Opal. But I don't know, those cliffs all about are mighty high. One slip could do you a lot more damage than any dirty cuss with food in his moustache, and I could give you back those rubbers if you like."

She shuddered in his arms. "He'd likely kill me anyway if I puked whilst he was trying to come in me. I ain't afraid of heights. But what about horses, honey?"

"I can't see hauling two ponies up those rocks," he said. "We'll have to leg it once we get to the top, and I have to tell you true, I don't know where we'll be when and if we do. If it's a flat-top mesa, we may be able to put some distance between us and them by the time we're missed. If it's all jagged rimrock, we won't. Either way, we have to have some firepower. What happened to those guns Banger and Will used to wear?"

"Slim's got 'em, I reckon. Do you want me to see if he'll let us have 'em?"

"Don't you dare," he said. "Slim's so reasonable he could be mistaken for friendly. But he's still one of the original Wild Bunch, and there's just no way you could convince him we aimed to shoot at cans in the dark. He'd know right off that we were planning to make a break for it. I'd a lot rather let Slim and the others sort of figure it out in the cold gray dawn, and that's still cutting it dangerously fine."

"Well, nobody's seen fit to take my guns away," she said, "and I'll be proud to share with you."

"We'd be in a lot better shape with one rifle between us. I might be able to make more than one rider keep his distance, given a rifle to work with. Fights at pistol range make me nervous even when the odds are only, say, ten to one."

She said, "Maybe we could sort of sneak about and see if anyone's left a saddle gun unguarded, honey."

He grimaced. "It might work. It might not. Once we make any move at all, the fat's in the fire. Adding up all the dangerous moves we could make, I reckon just climbing up and out with the two guns we know we have for sure beats pussyfooting about and maybe not finding any rifle anyway."

"Bueno," she said. "When do we start?"

"Let's give everyone a chance to settle down for the night. After midnight would be safer, but we need more time for our moonlight stroll. Ten sounds about right. It's pushing nine right now, so . . . Why are you at my fly again, Opal?"

"Hell, I gave you the rubbers, and you just said we have a whole hour, right?"

So even though he was sure it was the wrong way to get in shape for mountain climbing, they were soon undressed and at it again. She'd been right about the damned rubbers. Whoever made the Pasha brand no doubt made bicycle tires on the side. It took him so long that way, and she seemed pleased with the results by the time he managed to climax.

That is, he'd thought so. She wanted to do it again. "Later," he said. "If we get out of this mess alive, I mean to screw you silly. But let's save our strength for now. We've got a long hard night ahead of us."

She subsided in his arms, and as they cuddled, naked,

under the top blanket, she asked, "What happens then, Stuart?"

"After what?"

"After we get away and you screw me silly. How long are we talking about afore you move on to broader horizons and prettier gals?"

He kissed her. "Nobody's prettier than you...but, well, I do have a job, and I work out of Frisco."

"I've always wanted to see Frisco," she said. "I hear tell it's nice." He liked her even better when she added, "Someday I might get out that way. Would you mind if we run into one another out yonder someday?"

He assured her that sounded grand, and meant it. He knew he owed her at least the nearest town where she wasn't wanted and he could grub-stake her with some of the money he'd taken from those bodies back at the mine. It seemed only fair, since she'd shot them both.

Somewhere up the canyon a guitar was strumming and three or four voices were singing "Get Along, Old Paint" about as tunefully as alley cats or coyotes might have managed. Stringer propped himself on one elbow to observe that the scattered night fires all about were down to embers by now. It seemed likely that any nearby insomniacs would either wander up to join that song festival or start throwing boots at it ere long.

The sky above the canyon was now as starry as it ever got in these parts. At this altitude the bigger stars looked close enough to shoot down and the Milky Way ran from wall to wall of the canyon like a streak of silver paint airbrushed on black velvet. But all that starlight combined would not have been enough to outline some of the rimrocks above like that. So he knew the moon had made it above the Divide to the east by now.

"We'd best get dressed," he told Opal. "I don't reckon it will get much quieter around here than it is right now."

"It's still early," she protested. "Can't you do it to me one more time afore we leave, honey?"

He kissed her. "I'd be proud to, if we weren't leaving straight up a mighty steep cliff. Save some of that enthusiasm for a two-hundred-foot climb and at least fifty miles of hiking, and you'll have a whole lifetime of screwing ahead of you. If we get caught, you won't. I hope you understand this is a serious undertaking, Opal. You'd best stay here if there's any doubt in your mind."

She grimaced. "I was planning on talking Cousin Etta into going into a safer line of work even before Kid Curry shoved his bad breath and dirty moustache in my face. But you sure are a spoilsport. I wasn't planning on climbing any rocks with the part of me that still feels amorous."

He kissed her again, resisted the impulse to give her amorous parts a friendly feel, and reached for his jeans.

It didn't take them long to dress, once they'd put more amusing chores out of their minds. Stringer hung the one canteen that still held water across his chest with the strap over his left shoulder and the heavy canteen riding his right hip. But when he suggested wearing her gun rig as well, Opal protested that it was hers and wouldn't fit him as well in any case. He started to tell her to give him one gun to tuck in his waistband, at least, but then considered the risk of losing it as he scraped his belly over rocks, and decided the canteen would be awkward enough. Aside from the chagrin of dropping a .44-40 down a cliff, the noise it made would wake the dead, and he doubted anyone in camp had drunk that much yet.

He tried to check the time with his pocket watch, couldn't make out the dial despite the Milky Way, and said, "Well, if you're coming, we'd better get going."

As he helped her to her feet Opal asked which one of them should go first. "Neither," he said. "Without a rope, it makes no sense to climb in tandem. You don't want me falling on you and, no offense, I don't want you falling on me."

She gulped. "Jesus, do you reckon either of us is likely to, Stuart?"

He shrugged. "The wall looks solid. Most of the loose rock seems to have fallen ages ago. All the boulders I've seen on the floor of this canyon look well weathered, and I observed by daylight, riding in, that there didn't seem to be any scars of fresh rock on the cliffs all about."

She chuckled. "I admire a man who plans ahead. Are you sure you didn't make friends with me just to escape?"

He had, sort of. But she seemed reassured when he pointed out, "Hell, I've laid you twice and I still haven't escaped. I don't need you tagging along, damn it."

That inspired her to step off the tarp and up to the sheer cliff. She was four feet off the ground before he could get started.

Stringer found a nearby vertical crack, shoved a fist in as far as it would go, and twisted his wrist to wedge in solid as he found a toehold and started moving up. He called softly over to her, "Take it easy. The notion is to go up, not down. Test every new hold good before you put all your weight on it, and don't look down."

"Pooh," she said. "I guess I've scampered over rocks afore, and any handhold that can bear your weight ought to find it easier to bear mine, you big moose."

It wasn't easy, but he drew even with her. "We're not grabbing the same rock," he pointed out. "Slow down. I mean it. We've got one hell of a climb to go, and it's best to take it slow and steady."

She asked if that was the secret of his swell screwing,

and they moved on up, abreast, at Stringer's more cautious pace. They were both too winded, and a mite too far apart, for easy conversation. As he stared up the rock wall ahead of them, Stringer found it impossible to judge just where the canyon rim might be. There were too many bulges between. So despite his own advice, he looked down, and felt his balls trying to pucker up into his dry mouth. The ruby dots of scattered night fires told him they were already signaling an eight- or ten-story drop, putting him and the girl about halfway to the top, and he was already getting a cramp in the arch of his left foot.

He shifted his weight to free that foot and kicked the cliff a couple of times with his boot tip. It helped some, if not enough. Then, as he made ready to climb on, they both heard hoofbeats and war whoops down below, and some son of a bitch tossed more wood on a fire to shed more light on the subject.

"Freeze," he hissed across at Opal. "We have to play lizard on a rock right now. What in thunder could be going on down there?"

"More of the Wild Bunch coming in," she called back softly. "I told you Kid Curry sent word out. Lord, if that's my kin, Cousin Etta, coming in with Sundance and Butch—"

"I doubt that for more reasons than I've time to go into, and even if it's them, you can't climb down as easy as you can climb up, even in better light. You can study on it once we get topside. If they spot us now, they'll start shooting before they worry about what we might be doing up here. Start climbing again, and for God's sake, don't dislodge any pebbles."

He moved up another arm's length. But Opal gasped, "I seem to be stuck."

He swore softly and tried to keep his voice reassuring as

he called over to her, "Just take it easy. Thanks to that firelight, you ought to find it easier to spot the next handhold, honey."

She was trying to stay calm, but not quite making it. "There's nothing above me but a damned old bulge of bare-ass rock," she replied. "I'm having enough trouble hanging on where I am."

"You have to," he said. "Don't panic. I'll see if I can work my way over and give you a hand. The way up from over here looks possible."

He had to climb a few more feet in order to get his toes into the crosswise crack he'd been clinging to by his fingertips. He found higher handholds, albeit ominously wider apart, and said, "Hold on. I'm coming."

"I can't," Opal gasped through gritted teeth. "My fingers feel like I'm wearing empty gloves for hands and, Jesus, I'm getting leg cramps now!"

"Just move up and down a mite without trying to go anywhere. That ought to circulate your blood better. You have to hold on until I get there. So do it. It won't be long."

Then his questing right hand got to the bulge blocking the girl's route. She'd been right. There wasn't enough roughness to encourage a six-legged ant if it was afraid of high places. He worked his way as close as he could and looked down. Opal's form was a black outline against the faint orange glow from the canyon floor. He couldn't see her face, but he had no need to meet her frightened eyes when she gasped, "Honey, I'm about to go!"

He swung his right leg as far out under the bulge as he could and got as tight a grip as he could with his own numb fingertips. "Grab my ankle and hand on," he said. "I'll swing you under me, and you can grab the crack I'm standing in, see?"

"I can't," she answered in an agonized voice. "I only got one hand that still works, and it's all that's holding me right now."

"Bang the numb one on the rocks and wake it up, then. It's your only way out of that fix, honey."

He heard her slapping the hard rock with her soft palm. Then she gasped, "Oh, no!" and fell, screaming and falling, falling and screaming, for what seemed forever, until he heard her hit bottom. Neither her screams nor the ghastly sound of her landing had gone unnoticed down there.

CHAPTER
SEVEN

Stringer was climbing, cussing, and trying not to puke as the owlhoots started tossing more wood on their fires. One son of a bitch bounced bullets off the rocks all around before he could even see what he was shooting at.

Stringer was never to recall half the handholds he'd grabbed on the rest of the way up. He'd just climbed without looking for them, because he had to. He was three quarters of the way before he heard Kid Curry bellowing, "There he is, boys! It's that son of a bitching Stringer. I'll be vexed as hell with you all if he gets away!"

Bullets commenced to hit closer, and there was nothing like the notion of a bullet up the ass to inspire a man to all-out effort. He got peppered with spanged-off rock more than once. But before anyone down there had the sense to run for a saddle gun and do some sensible aiming at rifle range, Stringer was over the edge and running. He hadn't run far when he tripped over a slab of rock, skinned his hands, and sat up to get his bearings in such light as the moonlight offered.

He saw he was on an elevated flat dotted with moon-silvered short grass and clumps of what they called soap weed in Colorado and yucca back home. He didn't think he could be above the timberline, so the vegetation was likely sparse because bedrock lay just under the surface. Either way, there was no cover as far the eye could see.

On the other hand, one couldn't see all that far by moonlight, and there had to be cover somewhere. So Springer sprung back to his feet to go look for some. He forced himself to walk instead of run, and knowing they'd expect him to beeline south toward the rail line, he headed north. He knew they couldn't chase him up that cliff on horseback no matter how mad they were at him. He figured it would take a while before they worked their way to the top via some other canyon that wasn't a pure box. That told him he had some time to work with, though not how much.

He'd made it a mile or more to the north, across scenery he'd have found mighty tedious if he'd just been sightsee-ing, and then he was glad he was walking instead of run-ning, for he came close to walking off another cliff in the tricky light. Another canyon cut across his line of march. Kid Curry had known what he was doing, after all. This whole vast massif seemed to be Swiss-cheesed with can-yons, for what Mother Nature did in one place she tended to do in another.

He swung inland to work around the canyon barring his chosen escape route. It ran much farther into the rimrocks than the one the gang was hiding out in. When he found the ass end of it at last, he saw it wasn't boxed like the other one. If a man was dead set on getting down into it from the far end, he could sort of slide down safely

enough. Then Stringer considered men on horseback coming up the steep slope he'd found. He decided it was too
steep, and he had to go somewhere. So he lowered himself
over the four-foot slab of rimrock, found his boot heels on
dry scree that felt like railroad ballast and was just as
treacherous under foot, and proceeded to lower himself
into wherever. He'd no sooner done so when he heard a
distant shout, stuck his head back out of the crack at
ground level, and spotted a dotted line of torches to his
south. Not far enough to his south for comfort, even if they
had sense enough to spread out instead of riding in a bunch
after him before they'd guessed where he might be. He
hunkered down on the scree and started to half climb and
half slide down into the darkness.

It took forever to get to the bottom. When he did, the
exact bottom was hard to judge. The new canyon he'd
found was a lot skinnier than Kid Curry's, and choked with
fallen rocks as big or bigger than houses. He spent as much
time climbing as walking before things flattened out more
reasonable, closer to the narrow mouth. He took a swig
from his canteen. The night was cool, but it had still been
dry and dusty work. He could see why the Wild Bunch had
passed on such a disgusting canyon, even though they had
to know about it. That thought inspired him to recap the
canteen and start north again. There was no trail following
the base of the cliffs. But it did seem the natural way to
work north along them. So Stringer moved away through
the thicker scrub at an angle. He didn't want anyone
guessing the natural way he might walk, before he had a
horse and gun.

That was hot and dusty work as well. He kept tripping
over deadwood and bumping into bushes that smelled like
gin. When he found himself wandering through a tangle-
wood of second grown aspen in some ancient burn out, he

sat down on an old charred log to inhale some more water and study on what came next. It was harder to see where he was going, under the fluttering aspen leaves above him, and there were limits to how far north he might want to go in the first place. He knew that, save for mighty scattered spreads, there was hardly anyone living halfway honest between where he was and the original Hole in the Wall country. He knew he didn't want to walk that far on foot, even if both old Charlie Siringo and Deputy Lefors fell for Kid Curry's ruse and wound up there to greet him.

He resisted the impulse to roll a smoke as he mulled over that angle a spell. Curry couldn't have planned on meeting up with a dupe to feed the law red herrings. So from the very beginning the train robbers had been banking on the law expecting them to ride far, if not to their old hideout, instead of holing up so close. The important question was whether the law had bought the notion. That one posse he and poor little Opal had spotted sure had. Even if others had not, this was poor tracking country, and Kid Curry had been smart enough to work in the area as an honest or at least unsuspected cowhand for the last few months. So if he knew anything about tracking, and he had to, Kid Curry was in fair shape to put himself in a posse rider's saddle and figure where such a gent might look.

Stringer didn't know this neck of the woods as well as either. But he was good at putting himself in another gent's shoes or saddle. He sipped some more water and decided that if the box canyon was at all well known, to even local riders, Kid Curry never would have chosen it. Curry must have stumbled over it, chasing strays one day, and noticed that others who lived around there had never seen fit to explore the details of the ragged-ass range. Honest men hunting stock would be more likely to dismiss areas of bareass rock where no cow would want to hide out in the first place.

He brightened and told himself that his best bet now would be range a sensible cow might favor, areas honest local riders would know best. Kid Curry and the others would want to avoid them.

He rose and started working his way downslope, knowing what Colorado riders called parks and anyone else would call a mountain meadow tended to run north and south between the higher and more barren ridges. It wouldn't matter if he met up with a posse dumb enough to be searching for train robbers in green pastures. He just had to meet up with someone on his side of the law, fast. He couldn't tell if he was leaving sign with his boot heels, in this light. He suspected Kid Curry could track pretty good, by morning light, if he was.

There were limits to how hard even a lost and desperate man afoot and unarmed should push himself. So when the moon set in the wee small hours and Stringer found himself in a suddenly inky pine forest, he flopped down on the spongy pine duff for a catnap. It wasn't easy to fall asleep, even though he was tired as hell. He kept thinking about the way that poor little waif had screamed, falling to her death, and when he wasn't thinking about that, he was thinking wistfully about the brace of .44-40's she'd carried down with her and cursing himself for not having insisted on wearing that gun rig. It didn't help to tell himself old Opal would have been in just as bad a fix if he'd been the one to fall off that cliff. He tried to tell himself that last time they'd made love hadn't been the cause of her demise. He was still here, and he'd done most of the work.

He finally used a trick he'd long since discovered. He tried to think about something else that mattered less. He'd once managed to fall asleep down in Cuba with the Spaniards lobbing harassing rounds all night by considering how high was up, how long was forever, and which was more important. He tried it now, but was so tired and his brain so choked up with worries that it just scared him.

He finally lit on the gal on the second landing, back in Frisco. He generally tried not to think about her because he knew his own weak nature and that a man who messed with she-males where he lived or worked was just plain stupid. But the gal on the second landing sure was something to think about. She was an artist's model at that art school on Russian Hill. So she was no doubt used to letting people see her bareass. Only she sort of brought her work habits back to the boardinghouse they shared south of Market Street, and anyone could see those art students liked to draw her because she was built even better than that well-known brick edifice.

Stringer didn't recall her name or anything else about her, since he'd always made a point of just nodding politely and going on up the stairs to his own garret room when he passed her open doorway, where she posed bareass on her big brass bed like she thought she was Cleopatra and he was at least old Mark Anthony. He'd never been dumb enough to ask, of course, but he'd often wondered if she even noticed when she was naked or not, seeing she made her living that way.

This time he decided to go on in when she invited him so slinky with her great big bedroom eyes. He hung his Rough Rider hat on a brass bedpost and sat down beside her on the satin spread as she purred, "What took you so long, bashful?"

But then, just as he was trying to get it in, old Sam Barca was yelling at them from the doorway. The crusty, bald features editor didn't seem to notice both of them were naked or that Stringer sure had to piss bad. Old Sam yelled, "You were due at the office with that obit on Miss Calamity Jane Canary hours ago, and we had to go to press without it. You'd better have a good excuse for missing your deadline, Stringer!"

"I'd forgot all about her dying as the Widow Burke just recent, Boss," Stringer explained. "I thought you sent me to write up Pearl Hart, the bandit queen. This ain't her, neither, and excuse me, ma'am, but I just have to take a leak before I wet my jeans."

The girl on the second landing said, "You men are all alike, and you're not wearing jeans right now, you fool."

He proved her wrong by waking up, just in time, and watering a nearby pine. He shook his head wearily, deciding he'd been right about that sassy gal on the second landing. Even when you give in to her, she could still be a nightmare.

He was wide awake by the time he'd rebuttoned his jeans. He was just as glad, because whether the moon had decided to back up or whether the sun was sneaking up the other way, it was getting lighter now between the trees.

He put his hat and canteen back on and started walking the stiffness out of his bones. He was hungry as well as chilled. When he came to a grass-lined rill of sweetwater, farther down, he was still goose bumped under his denim duds, but he found some wild onions by the water, at least. They were more like bitty scallions than the onions one bought for serious eating at the grocery. But there were plenty of 'em, and they tasted sweet as real bermudas. So he ate a mess of them, drank the last of his water, and began to refill the canteen from the rill before he wondered why. The rill was running southwest through some trees and a lot of good green grass. He'd circled wide enough if he'd lost them and not far enough if he hadn't. Either way, the running water figured to lead to some town or at least some spread. He knew it was safer to follow it than to wander about in broad daylight until he ran into the Wild Bunch on foot without even that busted .32 handy.

He started to discard the canteen as useless weight. Then he had a better idea, and cut the strap free with his pocket knife. This left him almost six feet of supple leather to play with. It was smooth on one side and rough on the other. As he followed the running water, he kept running the leather through his hands, trying to remember that trick an Indian playmate had shown him so long ago in the sweet by and by of a Mother Lode childhood.

By experimenting with his knife while he kept walking, he was able to split the strap a little over halfway down its length, and yep, when he dunked the leather in the rill and worked a water-rounded rock into the split, it formed a sort of half-assed pocket. He kept walking and forming the leather over the stone until it began to dry in that shape. He'd put more muscle than water into the effort. He still didn't know if it would work.

The next time he paused to rest his legs, he sat on a boulder and split one end of the strap, forming a sort of wrist loop. He slipped his right wrist through it. He had to stand up again to find out if he knew what he was doing. It turned out he did, sort of, albeit old Larry Blue Basket had it down a lot better, even at the age of ten.

Stringer held the loose end of the thong in the same hand as he swung the rock in the pocket midway down the leather like a pendulum, until he could see it was willing to stay put. Then he took a deep breath, whirled the whole invention up over his head, and commenced to twirl the crude slingshot like a show rope until it was humming like a monstrous bee. He had no idea how Larry Blue Basket had aimed, but when he let go the free end, the pebble shot across the rill and into the trees on the far side almost faster than the eye could follow. Stringer grinned, stopped, and gathered a hip pocket full of pebbles from the rill, trying to keep them about the same size and to hell with the color.

As he moved on, firing rock bullets in every direction including some that surprised him, he could see why the ancient Romans as well as young David had thought so highly of this sport. For while no boys had bothered with this sort of slingshot since old Charlie Goodyear had learned how to make rubber back in the 1830's, the old-fashioned kind sure shot ferocious. Rubber bands could only store so much energy. A good-sized man whirling a good-sized pebble at the end of a yard-long loop could store up a hell of a lot more. When he accidently hit an aspen trunk at well beyond pistol-fighting range, Stringer walked over to regard the results and whistled. Then he muttered, "Poor old Goliath. He must have been dumb as hell if he went up against a Hebrew slinger in no more than a suit of brass armor!"

The quail-egg-sized pebble was embedded deep in the green bark and white wood of the aspen, and when Stringer tried to pry it out with his fingers, it didn't want to come. He decided it was easier to find another rock in the Rocky Mountains than to dig one out of a tree, and moved on, muttering, "Now, if only there was some damned way to *aim*."

He'd walked quite a ways and shot many a rock before he began to get the hang of it. It would have taken him longer if he hadn't already been a good roper. But he began to see that it was something like casting a loop of throw rope at a target, only different. You aimed a loop of rope above a cow to let it drop as it slowed down. Stones fired by a sling flew straighter and hardly slowed down enough to matter. When he passed through an open glade, he ex-

perimented with long range and whistled again, for he saw
he could lob a stone about as far as a pistol would shoot,
and you couldn't hit anything with a pistol at long range to
begin with.

All that slingshot practice had at least taken his mind off
his legs for a few miles. But both were starting to tire by
the time the rill led him into a thick tangle of alders and
black willow. He stopped in the heavy cover, sat down by
the water, and hauled off his boots.

The mountain water, born in the snowfields of the Rabbit Ears to the northeast, was so cold it numbed his tired
feet. That had been the general idea. He lay lengthwise to
drink some of the same, upstream from his feet. It wasn't
as easy as it looked. He had to take off his hat and press his
cheek to the grassy bank to get at the water with his lips.
When he did, it tasted better than some wine he'd drunk in
his time. Then he noticed the ear he had to the ground was
picking up dull thuds. Unless he'd discovered a species of
earthworms that used picks and shovels, someone was
coming, mounted, fast.

Stringer swore, hauled his bare feet out of the water,
and scooped up his hat and boots to move back into the
alders. He dropped his load and armed his sling. He'd of
course have never risked really using it had the approaching rider simply passed by. But to Stringer's dismay, when
a rider he recalled from the bunch who'd kidnapped him
from that club car came into sight, he sighted the sign
Stringer had left by the streambank and reined in to dismount and study it. Stringer didn't know if the sign he'd
left by crushing streamside grass led anywhere more important, but he knew he could sure use that rascal's pony
and Winchester right now. So as the train robber hunkered
down to poke at bent grass stems, Stringer wound up his
improvised weapon.

He would never know whether the bandit had spotted more sign or reacted to the odd whir of a spinning slingshot. Either way he was rising, and drawing, when Stringer let fly.

He knew he was dead if he missed. That may or may not have inspired his aim. The quail egg of white agate had an even more awesome effect on a human head than that other had had on a more solid aspen tree. The sound was that of a pumpkin hit by a blacksmith's hammer. The victim's eyes shot out of his skull to the end of their stalks. Then he was dyeing the stream red with his shattered head, and the pony he'd been riding was off and running.

Stringer ran after it, barefoot, yelling, "Come back here, horse!" Even as he saw that saddle gun and something less tedious to travel with was tearing upstream at a dead run. When they vanished from sight, Stringer sighed, moved back to where his victim lay half awash, and bent down to grab the dead man's boots and haul him out of sight amid the alders. Then he put on his own boots, hat, and the tie-down-holstered .45 Colt '74 old Larry Blue Basket's childhood skills had worked so well against. Stringer wondered if old Larry had used that trick in Cuba before Spanish shrapnel killed him near Santiago that time.

Stringer favored double-action for his own use, but the Colt '74, or Peacemaker, still had its admirers for good reason. It had a nice balance, and there was almost no way to bust up such a rugged sidearm. He put the few dollars the poor cuss had gotten for his part in the train robbery away, along with the slingshot. There were five rounds in the wheel and thirty-three in the loops of the gun belt, but as he'd just proven, a man just never could have enough weapons when the going got rough.

CHAPTER
EIGHT

Knowing the rider he'd just killed had come up the rill, Stringer didn't think it was a good idea to go any farther down it. He knew what the country he'd come down out of was like. He moved upslope the other way along the tree line in hopes that if the next draw over wasn't prettier, it would at least be farther from Kid Curry's hideout.

The ridge was more wooded than rocky along the top. There was a game trail following it. There almost always was. Deer and elk stayed among the trees by day and came out in the open at twilight to graze. He didn't want to meet any deer, elk, or outlaws scouting the local trails. So he moved down into the grassy park beyond, leaped the inevitable rill running down it, and worked his way to the tree line on the far side. Then he started south some more.

The trees hadn't been planted by anyone, let alone straight, between field and forest. So the cover zigzagged in a most annoying way for a man trying to get anywhere in a hurry. He cut some corners by bulling through prongs of the woods, mostly aspen or spruce, or by risking a short walk across open fingers of grass. Some patches of grass had been grazed recently, but none of the clumps or nettles had been cropped. That added up to cows instead of sheep. As he worked farther south, he saw ever more signs of grazing and knew he had to be approaching a cattle spread. A small one or a mighty distant one, judging by the sign. The grass was shortest down along the stream, where it would have grown longest and greenest, left to its own notions.

He worked his way through an aspen thicket to see that, sure enough, a dozen odd heads of scrub stock were lazing on the sunny open slope ahead. The tree line hairpinned way the hell up to the ridge line. He decided to beeline straight across. As he broke cover, a chongo-horned bull that had hitherto been reclining among its harem got to its feet to regard Stringer with interest.

Range stock of any lineage tends to consider a human being on horseback as something to run from while a human afoot can strike the bovine species as a novelty to have fun with. The chongo out yonder looked part longhorn and part Jersey, and as many a farmer or his widow can tell you, milk cows have been bred for producing lots of milk, not for sweetness of temper, and no Spanish bullfighter with the brains of a gnat would mess with a Jersey bull.

Stringer hoped the mongrel out yonder would take after its longhorn ancestors as he swung upslope to pass the critters sort of polite. Longhorns were as likely to spook as charge, and no bull likes to run uphill on a warm day. But the chongo must not have found the morning that warm or the slope that steep, for it put its tail up, put its head down, and came at him leatherbent for killing.

Stringer started to draw on the brute. Then he had a better idea and whipped out his slingshot. He didn't have time to swing it more than a couple of times, which was just as well for the both of them. The bull got a sudden headache and ran off bawling like a calf. So Stringer knew he wouldn't have to explain dead stock to its owner. As the cows jumped up to follow their lord and master to wherever the hell he seemed to be going, the relieved Stringer read a couple of brands as S Bar Diamond. The brands had been stamped, not worked in with a running iron. That read as an honest, businesslike outfit. Folk inclined to increase their herds more casual still favored running irons, no matter how the Cattleman's Protective Association frowned on the practice. So it seemed unlikely the S Bar Diamond, whoever they were, were in league with the Wild Bunch.

But the spread was harder to locate than its cows. Stringer passed more beef on the hoof, albeit not as ornery, and might have passed their owner's spread entire if he hadn't spied faint wood smoke rising above some treetops up the slope.

He headed into the trees a ways and had to circle some before he saw a cluster of low-slung log structures nestled in a semicircle of granite outcrops. He could see at a glance the layout took advantage of the lay of the land. The rocks shielded the main cabin and outbuildings from the winter winds, while the aspen out front shaded the spread in summer and went bare in winter to let such sun as there was warm the dooryard and corral. He didn't see any horses in the corral. But as he came closer, some chickens commenced to bark at him.

Pussyfooting up to an isolated cabin could be injurious to one's health. So Stringer waved his hat at the front windows in case anyone was staring out 'em, and strode across the dooryard to the long front veranda. As he got one foot up on the split logs, the front door opened a crack, the barrel of a ten-gauge poked out at him, and a feminine but determined voice told him he'd come just about far enough.

Holding his hat in his gun hand, Stringer told the shotgun muzzle, "My name is Stuart MacKail and I write for the *San Francisco Sun,* ma'am. I got kidnapped off a train by the Wild Bunch day before yesterday. Then I escaped, and now I don't know where I am."

"That well may be," the woman inside the cabin said, "but I'm a woman alone with both my hands off riding with the posse. Anyone can say they're anybody. But if I was you, I'd just keep walking south until you come to the railroad tracks. Once you find 'em, you can head either way. The creek running down this valley runs under the tracks about midway betwixt stops about fifteen miles apart."

He asked how far the tracks were and when she said half a day's ride he said, "I'm not riding, ma'am. Might you have a pony you'd be willing to sell?"

"I got one mount on the place right now," she said. "It's out back in the stable and it's mine. I can cover the stable door from my back window, so it's neither for sale nor for stealing, if you know what's good for you."

He sighed. "I can see how you wouldn't want to be this far from civilization without a mount, ma'am. I know it's been vexing *me* a heap. So let's study on the fix we could both be in. I know for a fact some armed rascals are out hunting for me, and you say your menfolk rode out and left you here all alone?"

She sniffed. "They ain't my menfolk. They work for me, or they did. I told 'em not to waste time with that fool posse when we've got chores to do around here. But some young rascals would far more chase after outlaws than help a poor old widow woman run her spread, I reckon. You could make the rail line before dark, if you started moving on about now."

"I don't think you've been paying attention to me, no offense," he said. "I know for certain that one of the Wild Bunch, at the least, was just over in the next valley, an easy ride from here, since I just walked it. I don't know where any posse might be just now, but the only one I know about was riding the wrong way. The best bet for the two of us would be to hole up in this cabin and wait until your hands get back. Sooner or later someone has to come by, and whether it's the law or the outlaws, we can greet 'em safer from inside, see?"

She didn't. "I ain't letting any strange man in. This scattergun is getting heavy, and if you don't light out right now, it just might go off, hear?"

Stringer put his hat back on and got out his wallet. "Look, I'll show you my identification."

But she shoved the gun muzzle further out at him. "Don't bother. It's as easy to take an honest man's wallet as his watch, once you take to robbing folk."

He sighed in resignation, and put his wallet away. Then, as he began to turn as if to leave, he grabbed the muzzle of her shotgun and pulled hard.

She pulled the trigger at the same time, and the ten-gauge made an awesome noise. But since he'd known better than to point a gun he was holding by either end at his fool self, the discharge only stung his hand. And then, since she'd been too stubborn to let go, she was sitting in the dooryard dust at his feet, blushing like a rose and trying to get her calico skirts down before anyone noticed she wore nothing under them and was blond all over.

The ten-gauge was single-shot, so he leaned it against

her cabin wall and moved out to help her politely to her bare feet. She let him, but called him a brute anyway. Then she said, "If you mean to rape me, try and do it more gentle than that. It's been a spell since I've been with any man, even willing."

He assured her of his good intent as she dusted herself off, and he noticed she was somewhat younger and not as tough-looking as he'd expected from her surly manners through a door crack. She was around thirty, give or take hard living and no recent trips to any beauty shop the Gibson Girl had ever visited. Her flaxen hair hung down in long braids on either side of her high cheekbones and slanty blue Slavic eyes. She was bigger in every way than poor little Opal, but her big-boned frame was firm from hard work, and for such a natural blonde, she tanned evenly instead of catching freckles.

Her thin blue calico dress, he now knew for certain, was all she had on. Her Junoesque torso hourglassed nicely, with no need for whalebone cinching. Her heroic chest measurements seemed able to defy gravity without any artificial help, either. He smiled at her. "As I was saying, the two of us together ought to be able to fort up behind those fine logs until help arrives, ma'am."

"God damn your eyes," she said, "you just dumped me in the dust like a sack of spuds, and I'll bet you tore my dress!"

She turned her back on him, pulling her skirts tight across her considerable but shapely rump. "Is any of me showing back there?" she demanded.

"No, ma'am. Not any skin, leastways. Hold still and let me dust you some back there."

She did, as he gave her a few good licks with his battered old hat. Then she giggled despite herself. "That's enough, you rough-handed thing. You can see I'm not carrying a watch or any valuables under this thin calico, so if you don't meant to ravage my fair white body out here, we may as well go on inside."

They did. He picked up her shotgun as they did so and put it back in the gun rack by her door before he shut the same, saying, "I hope you have more shells, just in case."

She'd moved to the far side of a deal table between the door and her cast-iron cookstove. She stared soberly at him in the dimmer light. "I must be getting touched in the head. I'm beginning to buy your story. You sure don't act like no outlaw."

He asked how many outlaws she might know, and she replied, "I've heard tell a cuss that's been working in these parts by the name of Tap Duncan was really Kid Curry all the time. He came by a month or so ago to ask if I needed any more help. I said no because it was true and because I didn't like the look of him, even before I found out he was wanted by the law. He wasn't half as polite and clean-cut as you. Say, you ain't Butch or Sundance, are you? They say both of them treats women polite, even if they do treat men sort of mean."

He started to reach for his credentials again, then decided she might feel upset if he proved for certain she couldn't read. "We're not going to get along at all if you keep taking me for one of the gents who may be out to do us both some dirt," he said. "So I want you to listen tight. Would I be out in these hills all alone and on foot if I was riding with the Wild Bunch?"

She shrugged. "Maybe not. But that tie-down holster sure looks odd on you if you're so innocent. I grew up near Dodge while it was getting famous for serious gunfighting, and lots of gents pointed out to me as killers never wore their guns serious as you're wearing that one."

"You'll notice I don't really have it tied to my fool

thigh," he said. "I never bought it. I took it off that Wild Bunch rider I just told you about."

"How'd you manage that?" she asked.

He shrugged modestly. "I killed him with a rock. I tried to hide his remains, afterward, and I don't think I left much sign in the dry grass and forest duff I've walked over since. But it wasn't far, and I don't see how we'd have met at all if he hadn't been hunting me. Do you have any long-range weapons around here, ma'am?"

"Not now," she said. "The boys rid off with my late husband's Henry and the Winchester one of 'em already owned. My name may as well be Tanya, seeing you don't work for me and may not be an outlaw after all. Have you et yet this morning?"

"Well, I found some wild onion at daybreak."

She smiled softly. "I noticed. I'd best rustle us up some steak and onions in self-defense. Set yourself down and mayhaps I can find us some cider as well."

Stringer hauled a three-legged stool out from under the table to do as he was told. As the big blonde bustled over her stove, he learned more about her. Her name was Tanya Dillinger. It was her late husband who'd been German. Her folk had been Russian immigrants who'd homesteaded down near Dodge in the '60s after the big war back east. Karl Dillinger had won this spread off a gent they called Sam Diamond in a game of high-stakes stud. Neither Dillinger nor his new bride had known, until they got up this way, that old Sam Diamond hadn't known much more about raising beef than playing cards. She bitched that, as Stringer could see, their spread was too cut up by wooded ridges to hold a big enough herd without hiring more hands than might be profitable. But by the time she and her husband had sold out and moved all the way up here, they figured they were stuck with the damned place. Sam Diamond hadn't even warned them about that part-Jersey breeding bull, and she said she was glad Stringer hadn't killed it, since it was the only bull she owned.

He asked if that might be the cause of her being a widow, and she didn't turn from her stove as she sighed and said, "No. It was another card game, in Hydrate, with a sore loser. They strung him up for me, of course. But I don't mind saying it ain't been easy running this spread on my own since I buried my man."

She brought the steak and onions to the table and put tin cups and a cider jug beside the main course. Her place servings were a mite rustic as well. But he'd eaten steak before with a bent fork and a paring knife, so he didn't complain. He hadn't realized until he dug in how hungry he'd really gotten since those beans in Kid Curry's camp. The rare steak and raw onions tasted grand. But when he went to wash them down with cider, he gasped in surprise. "How did you get this cider so hard, Tanya?" he asked. "I didn't notice a liquor still on your property, coming in just now."

She sipped her own ferocious drink like it was table wine. "Don't need a still in these parts if you're at all patient and temperate. We get the cider sweet in town in the fall. I generally get enough to last from one harvest to the next. Come winter time, say around Christmas, the cider's turned hard all by itself in the jugs."

He shook his head. "This stuff has been distilled to no-fooling applejack. Just left to ferment, it can't get much harder than wine. It's a simple law of nature."

"I don't have to run it through no still," she said. "I let Jack Frost distill it. It's a trick my daddy learned in the old country. He said in Russia lots of folk pour cider in tin buckets and let it freeze in the cold outside. It don't freeze solid, no matter how cold it gets. The water in the cider is all that turns to ice. So all you got to do is take the ice out and throw it away and what's left in the bottom of the bucket is more like brandy."

He laughed. "I noticed. It's small wonder you have trouble controlling your hired help if you've been serving 'em such fire water. Were they sober enough when they left to mention when they might be coming back?"

She shrugged. "I told 'em not to come back if they rid off like that with my best ponies and Karl's old repeating Henry. Neither one of 'em was worth spit to begin with. I should have known better than to hire sissy boys."

He washed down his applejack with the last of his steak. "I hope I have your permit to smoke. I sure need something cool in my mouth right now. How come you call them sissy boys? I'd call it mayhaps thoughtless, but hardly sissy, to go riding off after train robbers, Tanya."

As he got out the makings and started to roll, the big blonde explained, "They ain't sissies about fighting or even working, if I keep an eye on 'em. They're sissies about one another. I try to keep an open mind about what others may or may not do in bed, as long as it ain't with me. But I'm sure young Danny would have minded me and stood put here if that wilder Pete hadn't been so anxious to ride off with that posse. Pete seems to think he's some kind of hero, even if he does have a lover-girl everyone else calls Danny."

Stringer whistled softly, then licked the paper to seal it. "I can see why you might feel annoyed with 'em," he observed. "It's just another fact of nature that lots of cow drifters drift into that style of lovemaking. Hands don't get into town that often, even when they're good-looking and not shy about real women. You hear tales about certain riders in every cow camp. It isn't often that anyone lets such notions show, however."

He lit his smoke and shot her a thoughtful look. "It may be just as well, in this case. You're a mighty handsome gal. Things could have wound up even more awkward out here, alone with two young cowhands, if they'd felt more like most men do about even ugly women."

She grimaced. "I'd never let my help trifle with me. It's the wrong way to run an outfit. I hired sissy boys with that in mind. They had to come to me for a job, or fight better where they'd worked before. My mistake was that I figured it would be sort of like hiring a married couple. I didn't know they'd gang up against me when that silly Pete decided to go chasing after train robbers like a hero. Why on earth do you reckon a knowed sissy boy would want to be a hero in the first place, Stu?"

Her guest winced. "Call me Stringer. I know it's a dumb nickname but it still doesn't sound like cow-camp mulligan. As for old Pete's quest for glory, mayhaps he doesn't like being called a sissy boy. There's this brain doctor over in Vienna town who's been writing lots of stuff about such matters. He suspects a lot of men who dash about killing tigers and brushing their teeth with steel files could be sort of making up for the fact that they played the gal's part in boarding school before anyone told them how queer that sounded."

He took a cooling drag on his smoke and added, "Some famous fighting men never bothered to hide the fact that they liked boys as well or better than gals. I've never understood such ferocious fairies, but on the other hand, I've never seen any sense in looking for needless trouble to begin with. Mayhaps you have to be a mite crazy to be any sort of hero."

She rose from the table, moved over to the bedstead in one corner, and patted the counterpane at her side. "This is the only comfortable place to sit around here. For a man who just owned up to killing a gunslick with a rock, you sure talk modest, ah, Stringer."

He left his hat on the table, rose, and went over to join her on the bed. The rope springing sagged them closer together than he'd meant to sit. But she didn't move away. So he didn't either as he explained, "That was different. A man has to defend himself. The ones I'm confused about are the men who go out of their way to get in fights. Most men know how to fight. If they're at all good at fighting, they know how easy it is to get hurt, and even when you hurt the other gent, it's not as if it felt like making love or eating chocolate."

"I know what it feels like to make love or eat chocolate, as seldom as I've gotten to of late," she replied. "What does it feel like to kill a man? That's one thrill I've never had a crack at."

He shook his head. "It's not a thrill. Not if you got your head screwed on right. You just feel glad it was him and not you. Maybe you feel a mite sorry for him. I don't buy those tales of nightmares and remorse some old boys brought back from the war with Spain, either. I sometimes suspect that when a war vet weeps about having to do it because it was him or me, he's really telling you he was never in action. I had to kill a mess of Spanish soldiers down in Cuba a few years back. I wasn't even supposed to. But they paid no attention to my press patch, and after I'd done what I had to, I just thought they'd acted dumb and surly."

She suppressed a shudder. "I think men like you may be more dangerous in the end than the ones who brush their teeth with steel files. Have you ever made love to another man, the way Pete does to little Danny?"

He laughed incredulously. "I've never been in jail or out to sea that long. What difference would it make to you?

You'd have a time being a sissy boy even if you wanted to."

"I know," she said. "That's what I keep telling myself late at night, when I'm alone, here, and those two are out back in the lean-to, doing Lord knows what and enjoying it considerable from the way little Danny yells. Do you reckon I could be turning into a queer old gal, stuck up here in these lonesome hills?"

"No," he said. "But we'd best change the subject. For we'll likely be stuck here alone together some time, and it just so happens that I *do* like gals."

She lay back across the bed with a sad little sigh. "I like boys too," she said, "and it may be just as well we don't have no rubbers here. If we did, I ain't sure how long I could hold out."

He laughed and took off his gun rig. "You may find this hard to believe," he replied, "but it just so happens . . ."

But after they'd come that way together once, clothes and all, Tanya sighed and said, "Oh, take that fool thing off and let's do it right. Let me out of this damned old dress while you're at it."

He did, and while it was darker in her cabin than outside, he could still see enough to inspire him to renewed rising to the occasion. Her naked body was a passionate melody of curves and interesting dimples, and when he entered again—the way nature had intended—it was like starting fresh with a brand-new partner who, even better, had gotten over the first shyness. He was sure they were going to bust the ropes under her mattress as she pounded up as hard as he could pound down. But they didn't and when they'd finally climaxed with her somehow on top, she kissed him so hard it nearly bruised his lips.

"Oh, glory be," she panted." I didn't know I was that hard up, and I've been hard up as hell for a coon's age!"

He'd had another woman in a lot less time than she could be talking about, but he felt sincere when he told her she'd been on his mind this way before they'd ever met.

"I know," she said. "I've been dying for a man hung like you since before I got married, and I'd just about decided no man born of mortal woman could do it to me that fine!"

He rolled her off him, if only to breathe easier. "Let me get my second wind, and this day may not drag as much as we expected, after all." He cocked his head and added, "Those chickens outside sure are noisy."

"Screw the chickens," she said, "or better yet, screw me some more. I fed the fool birds hours ago. They've no call to fuss, unless they're jealous, you old horny rooster."

He sat up to reach for his duds and gun, saying, "Hold the sweet thought. I'd best have a look about. I've seldom heard chickens sounding off like that this close to high noon without a good reason."

She sat up and hugged him. "Just one more time and I'll let you get some sleep, honey. It's likely just a hawk. They fly over all the time. But they never swoop down through the treetops all about."

He gently disengaged from her embrace and stamped on his boots without the socks. "I'll do better by you in a minute if those birds are only clucking at a hawk. Is there a back way out of here, Tanya?"

She said there was no back door. But he found a rear window would do just as well in a pinch. He dropped out and dashed across such open space as there was between the cabin and the granite rocks it nestled amidst. He moved up a cleft to the pillow-shaped tops, .45 in hand, and had a good look-see all around.

He didn't see anything to worry about, and the chickens off to his right had calmed down as well. He glanced up at the sky, saw it was empty, and muttered, "Well, if it was a hawk, it gave up, and Lord give me strength. For the sun says it's still early, and that poor old Russian gal's been saving up for the rest of this very day."

Then he heard someone cough.

He'd only heard one. But it was enough. He eased off the rocks on the uphill side, away from the cabin, and on the balls of his feet started working his way through the dappled shade and juniper brush. As he eased around the last big boulder framing Tanya's spread to the east, he spotted Slim, crouched in a clump of brush with his Winchester trained on Tanya's front door.

Stringer moved into point blank range behind the lunger before he spoke. "Morning, Slim. I don't want to gun you, so why don't you just stand up slow, without that rifle?"

Slim didn't move or answer for a moment. Then he gently lay his saddle gun in the grass, as if he didn't want to get grit in the action, and slowly got to his own feet, hands out to his side. But as he slowly turned with a sheepish grin, Stringer saw Slim wore his pistol, low and ready.

"You sure are a good tracker, and I've seen you draw, Stringer said. "I reckon you'd better use your left hand to unbuckle that gun rig and let it fall natural, Slim."

"You owe me, Stringer," the gaunt gunslick replied. "If you was any sport at all, you'd holster your own gun and let us settle the matter fair, like friends."

"No offense, Slim," Stringer said, "but you wasn't pointing that Winchester friendly at that door across the yard just now."

"I wasn't aiming to bushwack nobody. We wasn't even sure you was in there. I was just covering all bets until the kid I sent for help could get back here with the others, see?"

"I do now," Stringer said. "I thank you for warning me that our stay here must be short and sweet. Now I got to tie you up. I got a fathom of canteen thong in a hip pocket as ought to do the job for us. But first I want that sidearm of yours on the ground."

"I don't want to be tied up," Slim said. "Put your own hardware in its holster and let's start even. You ain't afraid of me, are you?"

Stringer sighed. "There's a doc in Vienna town who might say you turned bad because you like to scare folk, Slim. I don't have to prove anything. So about that buckle . . ."

"I won't do it," Slim insisted. "You go ahead and shoot if you have to."

"Damn it, Slim, do I look like a cold-blooded murderer to you?"

"Nope," Slim said. "I was sort of banking on that. Ain't this fun?"

Stringer didn't think it was. He scowled as hard as he could at the grinning lunger as he tried to figure out what on earth he could do about their impasse. If he'd had more time to work with, he might have come up with something. As it was, all he could do was mutter, "Have it your way, then," and holster his own gun.

Slim nodded. "Thanks. That makes us even no matter how it turns out." Then he slapped leather.

Stringer was braced for it, and it was still close. As he drew and fired in one motion, Slim's gun went off to raise a geyser of dust between them. Then Slim was staggering backward, dropped his own gun, and fell flat on his back like a puppet whose strings had all been cut at once.

Stringer walked over to him to see what was left. Slim opened his eyes and murmured, "I thought I could take you. But, you see, I've been sick." Then he coughed twice and stopped breathing forever.

As Stringer hunkered down to get Slim's gun belt and ammo, the big blonde appeared in her doorway, naked, to yell fool questions at him. "Get dressed," he called back. "Now. We got to get out of here, if it's not already too late!"

CHAPTER
NINE

Slim had left a spunky-looking roan tethered among the aspen a hundred yards or so north of Tanya's spread. Horse apples and other signs told Stringer that Slim's fellow scout had beelined back toward Kid Curry's canyon hideout. Stringer hoped that meant the main body of the gang was still there. By the time he got the pony back to the cabin, Tanya had put on her boots, a split riding skirt, and a man's work shirt.

He told her to put on Slim's gun, helped her aboard, and handed up her twelve-gauge before he said, "All right, you take the lead and get us to town. I'll try and keep your treasures safe from the rear. But for land's sake, watch where we're going."

She waited until he'd mounted up with Slim's Winchester across his thigh, and they were off. He saw she was following a two-rut wagon trace that led south from her spread in line with the valley drainage. They hadn't ridden far when he noticed the sign of two ponies going down the trail ahead of them.

"This isn't going to work," he called out. "That rain we had night before last has tidied up this trail to where even I can see where your two cowhands and nobody else passed this way since then. Do you know of another trail that's not as easy to read?"

"I do," she answered. "Lots of slick rock and gravel. But it's out of our way if we're still in a hurry."

"We're in a hell of a hurry," he said. "But it's still better to get there slow than not to get there." So she swung off and they forded the stream to ride through grass a spell. As they topped the first rise, he looked back and saw that sure enough they were leaving sign in the wind-cured stubble her damned cows had left.

"Swing a mite north," he called out, "so's they'll think we're doubling back on them foxy or, with luck, take us for some of their own."

She did as she was told. They punched through some trees, went across more grass and water, another line of trees, and now that she had him turned around total on her rugged range, she pointed south again. "The nearest town is thataway."

She couldn't prove it by him. But as he followed her, he felt cheered by the fact he couldn't see any trail they were following. They were moving over slick rock with both ponies sliding and bitching about it some.

"Hold on," he called out. "You're pushing too fast. Do you recall a notch ahead where we have to ride through a mess of big old rocks?"

When she said she did, he replied, "It's time I took the lead, then. I know where we are now. I came up this trail going the other way with that poor cuss I just had to shoot. I thought at the time what a handy place those rocks would make for an ambush and, no offense, I suspect I may be harder to ambush than you, you pretty little thing."

As they rode on south, he saw no reason to tell her just how he and poor little Opal had explored the possibilities of those rocks ahead. Unlike a lot of women he'd met, Stringer never felt compelled to list each and every former lover who'd used and abused him. Even if he had been, old Tanya would no doubt want to get used and abused the same way if he told her it was possible. The notion of her big blond body lining that rocky nest Opal had found for them was inspiring him too much for comfort as it was. But no matter how much a man liked women, a real man had to show some common sense about the subject.

They topped a lesser rocky rise to spy the notched hogback ahead. He reined in outside of rifle range and stared morosely back and forth along the natural wall of rock. There had to be a way around. There were two ends to the Great Wall of China if you wanted to ride far enough. But they didn't.

"There's just no way to scout that rocky hogback safe," he said. "But hang back at least fifty yards, and if anybody blows me out of this saddle, ride like hell. I don't think they'll follow you forever if they get me. You don't know as much about them. Even Kid Curry ought to be able to figure that out."

She started to argue. He told her not to, took a deep breath, and rode across the shallow draw fast to make himself a tougher target or get it over with if that didn't work.

But nobody was staked out amid the rocks ahead. He made sure by dismounting and climbing to yet another hollow, topside. Then he stood up against the sky and waved Tanya in with his Winchester.

By the time she'd ridden into the cleft, he'd climbed down to rejoin her. He remounted. "I know the way back to civilization from here," he told her, then noticed the way her dapple-gray was favoring its near forehoof, and added, "Hold it. I fear your pony picked up a pebble with his frog."

But then Stringer saw the hoofprints Tanya had left in the dust and muttered, "Oh, boy. You've thrown a shoe."

"I know," Tanya said. "It was back on that slick rock. Old gray, here, was about due to be reshod. I meant to have it done the next time I went shopping in town. There's nothing we can do about it now."

Stringer stared soberly north at nothing much. "I wish you'd told me sooner. Do you remember just where that shoe might be right now, honey?"

She said she wasn't sure. He swore softly. "Never mind. I'm sure someone will find it. Let's move down the slot a piece so they can read it wrong when you switch saddles without dismounting."

She waited until he'd led her around a bend of the notch before she asked what on earth he was talking about. He reined in to explain. "That gray can likely carry your belongings the rest of the way, limping some. He can't carry you as well. So I want you to ride this roan and lead the gray."

"What will you be riding, then?" she asked.

"Nothing. When and if anyone trails us this far, they'll see they seem to be tracking the two of us and that one of us is riding a pony with a shoe missing. That ought to encourage 'em in more ways than one. Such a trail will seem a snap to follow, and even better, nobody aboard a limpsome pony could hope to outrun 'em all the way to the railroad line. As I recall with some dismay, it's over twenty miles from here to there, right?"

She said she'd never counted the miles but that she figured it six or eight hours, walking her mount most of the way.

He thought about that. "Yeah, it evens out if you bee-line. You won't be taking all those zigzags Kid Curry did to leave the law a twisted trail. Try to avoid that abandoned mine to the south. They use it as a way station."

She said she didn't know what mine he was talking about.

"Never mind. I should have guessed the regular trail was less twisted than Kid Curry's head."

Then he got his left foot back out of its stirrup, reached out to step on a handy boulder instead, and swung out of the saddle with just the Winchester and a canteen Slim had hung on the roan. Handing the reins to Tanya, he told her, "Swing aboard. Hand me that shotgun first."

She didn't. The big blonde was as good aboard horses as aboard a bed, and made the switch easy enough. But she was crying as she told him, "You can't stay here alone and afoot, you fool. They'll kill you for certain."

"They weren't able to do that when I was afoot with just a slingshot," he said soothingly. "Now I've got a rifle and sidearm. So you just *vaya con Dios,* you pretty little thing, and I'll make sure you're not followed."

She dimpled and asked if he really thought she was a pretty little thing, adding, "Most men find me sort of awe-some."

He laughed, told her that was what a gal got for messing with shrimps, and then slapped the roan's rump with the barrel of the Winchester. Tanya was off before she could argue about it anymore.

By the time she'd have made it out the far side of the slot, Stringer was atop the rocks, looking about for a place to fort up. He found another sandy hollow that, while not quite as cozy as the one he'd shared with Opal somewhere to the south, covered the trail from the north just right. Wanting to let them guess where he was instead of spotting him, Stringer flopped down in the sand, removed his hat, and propped the Winchester through a handy cleft in the pillow-shaped granite rimrocks.

A million years or at least an hour went by without so much as a bird chirp to distract him. It had to be past high noon, but not enough to keep the sun from trying to fry him in the pan of rock he lay prone in. The thin mountain air dried his sweat as fast as it leaked out of him. The water in Slim's canteen tasted warm and tinny. The only thing to be said for his discomfort was that it kept him awake. Thanks to Tanya and the little sleep he'd had since leaving the Wild Bunch, his bones, at least, felt weary as all get out.

Another million years went by. The bright sunlight was playing tricks with the air currents above that lower rise to his north. He paid no mind to the dark rocks that seemed to float in air up yonder until he noticed they were getting even higher. Then he snapped to full alertness and saw they weren't rocks, but more like heads and shoulders. Then there were eight riders lined up on the rise, the legs of their mounts cut off at the knees by the shimmering mirage. One was pointing right at Stringer with what had to be a horseshoe in his free hand. Stringer knew they were more than likely just talking about the trail through the notch to his left.

"A little knowledge can be a dangerous thing," he growled. "You boys just come within range and we'll see how smart it was of you to find that loose shoe."

They did. Being wild and in a bunch, the Wild Bunch riders no doubt felt more than a match for any two riders, even if they'd failed to guess that one was a woman.

It wasn't easy, but Stringer waited until they were more

than halfway across the draw between them, then let his breath half out, held it, and squeezed off the first round with his sights trained on the lead rider.

The results were gratifying. Stringer had never fired that particular saddle gun before, but as he'd hoped, old Slim had sighted it right. The first owlhoot he fired it at did a backward somersault off his pony, spooking it considerable, and then Stringer was levering round after round into the milling mass of spooked riders and the dust they were raising as they all tried to be somewhere else without knowing exactly where that ought to be.

A voice that sounded like Kid Curry's shouted, "Back to the canyon! There's too many of 'em!" as Stringer emptied a couple more saddles and tried to figure which of the bastards could be the leader he really wanted the most. Then they were out of range, the sons of bitches, save for the four he'd put on the ground.

"That'll learn you," Stringer said as they vanished over the far rise. Then he checked to see how many rounds he had left in the Winchester's tube.

He had four. That was better than none, but he still wished the gun belt he'd taken from that other train robber had been stuffed with .44-40's instead of .45 shorts. He knew that was the reason a lot of the old-timers still wore pistols chambered for the same rounds as their Winchesters. The size of the hole one punched in a bastard didn't matter half as much as one's ability to punch lots of them. You'd think men riding with the Wild Bunch would pay attention to such details. But on the other hand, anyone professional enough to think ahead worth spit had no business riding with such a wild bunch.

It was getting easier to see why so many of the original Wild Bunch had dropped out of it of late. Putting all the outlaws in the area in one basket for the law had never struck Stringer as a great notion in the first place. The world was getting just too modernistic for such notions. What with the country out here more than half mapped in fair detail, a man had to study some before he took to the owlhoot trail. The day was about done when a boy could dream of being a bandit when he grew up and just go on and do it. At the rate things were going, it was going to take some book learning to be a crook. Some lawmen were already reading books about catching crooks. Over to France a lawman called Bertillon had even worked out ways to identify crooks who tried to change the way they looked, and some Englishman named Galton had convinced Scotland Yard that nobody in the world had the same fingerprints. He'd figured it out in '91, just three years too late to catch Jack the Ripper with the newfangled notion.

Stringer waited, hot and itchy, and then after a while a crow came down to walk around one of the bodies out there a couple of times before it went for the eyes. That encouraged some more old crows to come down and join their scout. It hardly seemed likely even crooks would just sit there and watch crows savage dead comrades. But Stringer still waited until the crows were acting just awful before he eased down from his ambush and gingerly moved out across the open battleground. Nobody pegged a shot at him from the rise to the north. He waved his hat at the crows and the nasty birds flapped off a few yards to cuss at him. He helped himself to both .45 and .44-40 ammo, along with such money as he found on gents in no condition to spend it. Then he told the crows the rest was all theirs and legged it back to the rock cleft.

He decided old Tanya had a good enough lead by now. The ones he'd chased the other way would hardly be dumb enough to ride the same way again, whether he was covering the cleft or not. But the way he'd do it, if he was Kid Curry, would be to work around to the far side and move along atop the rocks himself to see who was acting so mean in these parts. So, either way, it was no doubt time to leave these parts entire.

He was, damn it, afoot again. But at least he had two guns and plenty of ammo now, and thanks to the way he'd helped himself to more than one train robber's share, he no doubt had more money to show for that robbery than anyone who'd robbed the fool train.

It had been all very well to tell Tanya to beeline it. She knew this country. Stringer didn't. So he was forced to backtrack the only way he knew, along the crooked route the crooks had led him. A lot of it was downhill, and he and Opal had led the ailing Slim most of the way at a walk. So while horses took bigger steps than even a man Stringer's height, he figured he was making about the same time by jogging down slopes and walking up them. He forced himself to sit down and rest a few minutes at least once an hour. There'd been some discussion about that when he'd been covering an infantry outfit in Cuba once. Some crusty old-timers held that it was best to stay on one's feet the length of a forced march because once you were off 'em, it seemed harder to get back up again. But the army had made scientific studies, marching one outfit against another it couldn't compare notes with, and decided that while it was a close call, it did seem men who took trail breaks made up for the lost time by managing to walk instead of stagger the last few miles.

It still took hours for Stringer to notice he was moving down into that abandoned mining area. He was still high on the north slope of the valley when he spotted the half-dozen ponies tied up in the shade of the ruined stamping mill. The afternoon shade was getting darker and longer now. He hunkered down in the tall grass, squinted hard, and still failed to make out any human form down around the mine. But ponies hardly ever tethered themselves to anything. The afternoon sun, though lower, was hotter than ever. The riders had no doubt sought shelter in the mine itself.

That didn't mean any number of 'em couldn't pop out of the adit like armed cuckoo birds at any minute of any hour. Since he had no way of knowing which side of the law they might be on, he figured it would be best to sort of work around them. That part seemed easy enough. But, damn, he was sure tired of walking, and any one of those tethered mounts would fix him up just fine.

He could see they were lined up within easy view of the mine adit, and whether their riders were law or outlaw, they had to be smart enough to have someone posted as lookout. There had to be a better way. For all he really knew, the rascals holed up in the mine were posse riders, and he was in enough trouble without a charge of horse stealing to explain. The state of Colorado still hung horse thieves.

He couldn't just walk up to the mine adit and twist a door bell. But there was always the chance that no one else knew the way to the back door. Opal had been the only member of the Wild Bunch he'd ever told about that hole farther up. He nodded, eased back up over the rise, and made tracks. Once he judged he was out of line with the adit, he moved back over the ridge and made for the hole he and Opal had admired. Nobody had spotted him by the time he flopped facedown in the grass with his head staring straight down the murky shaft. He sniffed and detected wood smoke and . . . perfume?

Somewhere below, a high-pitched voice that jibed with

violet stink-pretty was bitching about something. He couldn't make out what she was saying. That meant she wasn't directly under him. A male voice answered, even more distorted. That meant he was not as deep in the mine as the gal, and when she bitched again, she seemed farther away. So Stringer lay the Winchester in the grass and started easing down the sinkhole to see who she was and what she was bitching about. Old Tanya had smelled more like onions than violets, and he'd have seen her dapple-gray out front if she'd made it to a posse holed up in a mine for some reason.

Getting down safely was easier to consider than to manage. But Stringer made it most of the way before he dislodged a fist-sized rock with his boot and sent it crashing down on the rocks below.

He froze, clinging to the walls like a bat, wondering just how a man in such a ridiculous position could draw a side-arm if he had to in a hurry. But as it turned out, he didn't have to, yet.

A female voice called out, "What was that?" and some gent, bless him, replied, "A falling rock, of course. You *saw* them rats around the remains of old Banger and Will, remember?"

She sort of sobbed she'd never forget, and Stringer was glad he'd left the bodies between the rock pile and the entrance. If they knew who the dead men were, they had to be Wild Bunch. It was still up for grabs what even gals who rode with bandits were doing in this hole in the ground.

Stringer lowered himself the rest of the way as quietly as he could. But when a rock crunched under him as he eased down off the rock pile at the bottom of the cave-in, that same sharp-eared she-male called out, "Listen! There's somebody back there, I tell you."

But this time it was another gal who told her, "Sure it is. Which one of them rat-eaten cadavers do you figure just got up, boogy-boogy-boogy?"

"Somebody ought to go back yonder and make sure we're alone in here," the first gal protested.

The male who'd spoken before laughed. "You just do that, Shirl. My ears is still ringing from the scream you gave when you went back there to take a squat and seen them two dead boys. I warned you not to go deep in this mine. It's old and half rotted and filled with rats. Big ones, judging from all the noise they're making. It's the front end of this hidey-hole we got to worry about. How are we doing out front, Tom?"

"So far so good," a more distant voice called back.

Hunkered as he was against the blackness of the mine, Stringer could make them out, sort of, against the daylight from the adit and the glow of the small fire they'd built on the ashes of the last one.

There were two men and four women. The outlaw whores and one man were easy pickings around the fire. The one posted near the exit was the problem, cuss his cautious hide.

Then one of the gals, bless her, called out, "These spuds look done, Tom," and the lookout turned to walk back and join them at the fire. Stringer recognized him by the orange glow as the trader, Tom, who'd brought corn liquor and doubtless other items of luxury to the canyon camp. It was now more obvious what they were doing here. Kid Curry hadn't made enough on that last train robbery to buy undivided loyalty.

Stringer rose, .45 in hand, to move up the shaft toward the fire. He didn't make enough noise for even the sharp-eared gal to detect. But since he and Tom were facing one another from opposing sides of the fire, Stringer could only get so close before the trader spotted him looming against the darkness like a ghost. So then old Tom acted dumb as hell.

Stringer fired as the older man slapped leather. The noise was deafening in the confined space, and all four gals screamed even before they could have noticed old Tom lay dead on his back like that. "Freeze!" Stringer yelled, and then, as all five of them did, he moved through his own reeking gun smoke to cover the now terrified survivors.

He saw that the remaining male with the painted bawds was the young wrangler from Kid Curry's camp. He nodded pleasantly. "I owe you, boy, and I was brought up to be polite to ladies. So just unbuckle your gun rig and we may be able to work something out."

The kid did as he was told. As he tossed his gun rig far away, like something disgusting, he almost sobbed, "Don't kill us, MacKail. None of these gals are packing guns, and I never took no actual part in that train robbery."

Stringer nodded. "That's what I just said. How many other camp followers have lit out by now?"

"Just about everyone who could," one of the whores said. "Kid Curry's acting crazy. I've never pulled a hold-up in my life, and even I can see that box canyon he's forted up in is a death trap!"

Stringer nodded again. "He's no doubt hoping the law won't find him there. But I admire your common sense, ma'am. Did I hear mention of spuds just now?"

The nearest whore hastily raked a couple of potatoes from the hot coals with a stick. "They're all yours," she said, "if you want 'em. I've somehow lost my appetite all of a sudden."

Stringer left them where they were, to cool for now, and told them all, "I think I see what you folk were planning. It was sort of dumb. When you're not wanted serious by the law, it's best not to meet up with a posse after dark. Do any of you have wanted paper posted on you, direct?"

Even the kid shook his head. "There you go," Stringer said. "No posse chasing train robbers is likely to waste much time on a mess of whores and their pimp. I'm sorry I have to put it that way, but that's what you look like and that's what you'll let 'em take you for if you've a lick of sense. Cut this sneaky act and ride direct for civilization by broad day while there's still some left. You're not half as likely to get shot by mistake as if you bump into anyone in the dark. I haven't time to make up stories for you. You can no doubt make up your own as you ride. I want you to start now. Ladies first."

As they all got to their feet, Stringer herded them out the adit. Then he told the young wrangler, "Leave Tom's mount here and get out of here pronto with the gals and the other ponies. I haven't time to waste on moral lectures either. So let's just hope you learned a good lesson, son. Since I don't know your name, I won't be able to tell the law how silly you've been acting. But keep it up and sooner or later you won't be so young and pretty, and someone like me is sure to blow you away. I want you to study on a parting comment I have to offer, between now and the next gun you pick up. I just got the drop on you, easy, and I'm not even a paid-up peace officer."

The young wrangler said he followed Stringer's drift. So the tall newspaperman waited until the five of them had mounted up and ridden on. Then he ducked back inside, got the crooked outlaw trader's money belt, the spuds, and rode on himself, aboard the dead man's fine chestnut gelding. He'd figured old Tom would be riding the best pony in the lot.

• • •

Stringer only remembered the way he'd come north, more or less, with the train robbers. So he was looking for that white-water stream, hoping it would be easier to ride up than down, when a long ragged line of other riders broke cover from the spruce ahead. He could see why they weren't worried about him. There had to be close to fifty of them. He became less worried when he spotted sunlight glinting off vest badges and noticed at least one of the posse riders was, for land's sake, riding sidesaddle.

He reined in and raised his hands politely before anyone could yell at him to do so. His lonesome as well as reasonable attitude seemed to mollify them some. Nobody shot at him as they closed in to circle him, although a couple made surly remarks about ropes and oak trees they'd passed just recently.

Before too many could agree to the notion, Stringer called out, "I was on that train, not robbing it. My handle is Stuart MacKail and I'm a stringer for the *San Francisco Sun*. I can prove it if you boys won't shoot me for reaching for my wallet."

The thick-set individual sporting a county badge on his greasy leather vest said, "You can tell your tale to the judge, stranger. We ain't got time to waste, and now you'll be riding with us cuffed to the horn as we check out an old mine one of the cowhands from around here just recalled."

"They're not there," Stringer said. "I know where they are, or at least the hard core of the gang. But I'm not sure I want to tell you, if you're going to act dumb. Kid Curry is mad at me. I'm not going anywheres near him, hand-cuffed."

The possed leader stared thoughtfully at him, then sighed. "Well, I hate to drag a man along a rock trail. But as you say you knows where Kid Curry might be right now, you're just going to have to tell us, and it's up to me to decide who wears handcuffs or not in these parts."

Things might have turned out uglier, had not the lady riding with them moved up the line just then to dimple at Stringer sweetly. "It's all right, I know this man," she said. "Like me, he's a member of the Fourth Estate."

The posse leader sighed. "I don't know what estate you live on, Miss Doyle, but I sure wish you'd go home. Like I keep telling you, this is a manhunt, not a picnic. You say you can vouch for this saddle tramp, ma'am?"

Kathy Doyle of the *San Francisco Examiner,* cuss her pretty hide and paper, sweetly replied, "Stringer and I have been professional rivals for some time. The last time we were on the same story, he scooped me, the mean thing. But that's all right. I think I'm two scoops ahead of him."

The burly deputy scowled. "Are we talking about newspapers or ice cream?" Then he turned to Stringer and growled, "All right. But if I don't handcuff you, will you talk some sense to this little lady, ah, Stringer?"

Stringer regarded Kathy Doyle more morosely than most men were inclined to, before they'd noticed how willful she could get. The pesky reporter from the infernal *Examiner* looked more like a real Gibson Girl than most of the young gals trying to. Right now she had a bitty black derby perched atop her upswept auburn hair, and her English riding outfit looked out of place in, for God's sake, Colorado. But despite her cameo features and slender build, there was a mighty stubborn set to her Celtic jaw. Stringer had seen her green Irish eyes blaze tiger ferocious one time, as he'd tried to stop her from beating up a longshoreman on the Barbary Coast back in Frisco.

"I can't promise anything about this pretty sass, pard," he told the deputy. "Bigger men than me have tried and failed. Meanwhile, if you boys want to get to Kid Curry before sundown, we've got some riding to do."

So they rode. Now that Stringer had been wandering about these parts for some time, he had the grain of the land set better in his mind and was able to beeline for that canyon area. During a short trail break, one of the local cowhands protested that they were hunting snipe with night coming on. "There's nothing out thataways but badlands and bad water," he said. "Besides that, when that rascal was working with us as Tap Duncan, it was way the hell south of here. He'd have had no call to hunt strays up this way."

"I won't argue that," Stringer replied. "He wasn't hunting strays all the times he might have said he was. He was hunting for hideouts and, like you, he figured no local riders would know much about badlands no sensible cow would be interested in. I know where we are now, and I know where that canyon I told you all about is. If you boys want to turn back, I'll be proud to turn back with you. I'm not about to go after the Wild Bunch alone. If I thought I could take 'em solo, I wouldn't have been running from 'em when I run into you. Kid Curry owes me for a friend of mine."

The burly leader growled, "The rascal owes lots of folk for lots of friends. I figure he'd have at least forty notches on his gun if growed men really went in for that notion. Let's go. Our brutes can rest once we get there."

They rode on, with Stringer in the lead, or trying to be. When Kathy Doyle fell in beside him again he sighed and told her, "I sure wish you'd hang back, Irish. It's not even safe in the rear, but at least you'd have a chance if we ride into an ambush."

"Pooh," she said. "I'm wearing a .25 under my garter, and I'll have you know I know how to use it."

He shook his head wearily. "For God's sake, leave it there. The law wants to hang Kid Curry, not tickle him to death. Are you sticking so close because you're afraid I'll scoop you on this story, Irish?"

"Won't you, if you get the chance?" she replied.

"It would serve you right," he said. "Girl reporters have unfair advantages even when they're not as crazy as you. But look, I'll share the story with you if you'll hang back out of my way like a sport. I know lots of things about the Wild Bunch that you'll never find out on your own, see?"

"I want to be in on the kill," she said.

"This isn't a fox hunt," he told her. "The lead riders are as likely to be killed as the rascals we're hunting. Everybody riding with us will know who got killed, by the time it's over. Act sensible and I promise we'll both file good stories together. As I said, I picked up some background material while the gang was holding me."

"Well, if you promise," she said. "But what if they shoot you before you can tell me?"

He laughed. "Think of the scoop you'll have then."

She reined in, but called out after him, "Be careful, you big goof."

He was. He reined in on a rise well out of rifle range from the canyon mouth. "That's it," he told the others. "It gets wider inside. The last time I looked, they had a lookout posted near the entrance. But the light's starting to get tricky, and if we move in afoot, with the sun dazzle behind us as we work from cover to cover, we ought to have 'em boxed by sundown."

The posse leader asked what was to stop them from getting out the back way.

"I've told you," Stringer said, "more than once—they're boxed. It's a box canyon, damn it."

"You say you got out of it, though," another rider said.

"I had to," Stringer replied. "But that's a good point. I know how to get up on the rimrocks on foot. Just a handful of us could make sure nobody climbs out the back way. If I was to, say, drop a rock down the cliffs for their amusement, I don't reckon any of 'em would even try."

The posse leader frowned thoughtfully. "We'd best all stick together until we know for sure they're really in that canyon. You said yourself, on the trail, that some of 'em, at least, have lit out in every direction."

Stringer nodded. "I think we could be talking about just Kid Curry and a handful of his more serious followers. If they've lit out as well, all I can say is that I'm sorry and that I tried."

"I'll find out," the posse leader said, and spurred his pony forward before Stringer could stop him.

When Kathy Doyle started to ride after him, Stringer caught her mount's bridle and stopped her, saying, "Not if I have to turn you over my knee and give you that spanking you should have had a long time ago!"

The posse leader wasn't as dumb as she was, after all. He reined in about three hundred yards from the canyon mouth and stood in his stirrups to bellow, "All right, boys, we know you're in there. So what's it going to be?"

A rifle round spanged dust too close to his mount's hooves for any sensible man to stay there. So he rode back to the rest of them, shouting, "Hot damn, sorry, ma'am. I just proved one mean-hearted gent's holed up in there, and that's good enough for me. How many boys do you reckon it will take to secure the rocks up yonder, Stringer?"

Stringer patted the stock of his Winchester grimly. "I've been studying on that. Kid Curry's only chance now is a bust-out right through you boys. He might be dumb enough to try that, once he sees he has no way out. If he does, you'll need all the firepower you can muster down here. I know the way, no horse can follow me, and if one rifle can't stop men from climbing sheer cliffs, no rifles can. So I'd best get going, alone, before anyone in there decides he's a human fly."

Nobody argued. Stringer dropped down the far side of the rise to ride on, unseen from the canyon mouth the posse had covered.

He hadn't ridden far when he noticed Kathy Doyle was riding with him. He didn't have time to argue. He knew she'd never in this world be able to climb after him in that long riding skirt once it got steep enough, and it would serve her right for being such a pest.

CHAPTER
TEN

As Stringer had noticed coming down off the mesa, the other canyon had likely been dismissed by Kid Curry to begin with because it was a bitch to explore. When he reined in just a few yards up it and began to dismount, Kathy Doyle joined him and asked how come. Stringer tethered his chestnut to a clump of sage with a little cheat grass growing close enough for the pony to mess with, if not enjoy.

"It's a mighty tedious climb from here on up," he told her. "But I'm hoping those owlhoots were too lazy to find out you can get to the top this way. You'd best go back to the others now. No telling how many snakes are denned among all those rocks ahead."

It didn't work. She dropped gracefully down from her side saddle. "Pooh, at this altitude?" she said. "You'll not get rid of me that easy."

Stringer didn't answer as he unlashed Tom the trader's

bedroll and canteens. Along with the Winchester, it made for an armful. Kathy asked if he was planning on home-steading atop the mesa.

"Might be stuck up there overnight," he tried. "It can get cold up there after dark."

She said, "Oh," and began to unfasten the roll and sad-dle bags from her own rig.

"Damn it, Irish," he said.

"Damn me no damns," she replied. "I rode all this way for a story, and you don't have to worry about me. I can look after myself. Lord knows I've had to, growing up on North Beach."

"Look," he said, "I can't manhandle you and all this gear over the rocks ahead, and some of them get sort of ferocious. Worse yet, if you get stuck halfway, you'll just have to stay stuck for quite a spell. We don't have much light left to work with, and that means you could wind up spending the night, alone, stuck on a rock in a dark spooky canyon."

"I'll shoot myself," she said. "Get going. You're right about it being close to sundown."

He swore, tethered her horse for her—since she didn't seem to have the brains to do it herself—and took the lead. The climb wasn't so bad at first. That gave a man time to think. As he did so, he chuckled and called back, "All right, you got me to tether your mount for you, Cleopatra. But from now on you're on your own. Watch that slab of sandstone between us, it's trying to be a rocking chair, and damn, there I went and did it again."

She laughed. "What's the use of having womanly charms if a girl's not allowed to enslave you brutes with them? How much farther do we have to go?"

"We haven't even started," he said. "No fooling, Irish, this is no place for the fair sex. Why don't you be a good girl and go back to the others? They're a lot more likely to see real action than I am."

"I've been riding with them for two days, MacKail, and all I've seen them do so far is spit tobacco juice and stare down at the ground. Who do you think you're fooling? From up top we'll have a bird's-eye view of the whole affair. Damn, I wish I had a camera. Maybe one of those motion picture ones Edison makes. I don't think anyone's ever made a motion picture of a real wild west gunfight. Do you?"

He chuckled. "A lot of 'em would no doubt go down in history different if they were recorded on film. Most of the famous shootouts, so far, have been written up by reporters who weren't there and had to take the word of the winning side. I've seen some nickelodeon versions of our national Iliad, and having seen the real thing as well, I had to chuckle some."

She tried to follow him over a big boulder, swore like a man, and hoisted her skirts shockingly to rejoin him on the far side, gear and all. "What are you staring at?" she asked. "I told you I was packing a garter gun."

He chuckled. "I can't wait till we get to some worse places I know of, up ahead. I hope you're wearing under-drawers."

"Why?" she asked. "Are you afraid you'll see something neither of us has ever seen before? Keep moving, damn it. I don't like the looks of that sky above us."

He glanced up as he kept climbing. The sky was almost cloudless, but the few bits of fluff they could see from the canyon bottom were blushing as if they'd peeked up Kathy's skirts as well. He told her, "Sunsets last a spell at this latitude and altitude. It won't be really dark until after nine. Hand me those damned saddlebags. You're never going to make it with that load, and it's too late for you to turn back now."

She dimpled up at him as she passed the twin bags over a big rock to him.

"I know," he said. "Even when we know the fair sex is doing it to us, we just don't know what to do about it."

"Sometimes *we* don't either," she replied. "Help me over this rock, damn it."

He did. Her small delicate-looking hand was as strong as many a man's as she clung to his and hooked a shapely leg and high-button shoe over the boulder. He couldn't be sure, in this tricky light, but if she was wearing underdrawers, they had to be mighty short and dark. As they moved up a less awkward stretch, she asked, "Do you mind if I ask you something about yourself I've never been able to fathom, Stringer?"

"Shoot," he said.

"I've read your stuff. It's good, even if you do work for the *Sun*. It's literate too. You even use words like Iliad when you don't think any cowboys are looking."

"So what?" he replied. "I took a degree in English Lit at Stanford, and my editor, Sam Barca, gives me hell when I spell dumb."

"But you talk like a cowhand," she said. "How come?"

"I was raised as a cowhand. How else would you expect me to talk, with your Irish brogue?"

"Don't be silly," she almost snapped. "I don't have a brogue, and I'll have you know I speak the King's English with proper grammar as well!"

He helped her over another rock as he chuckled. "All right, you talk good English with a touch of the blarney. My point is that it doesn't show, in writing. Nobody writes the way they talk or talks the way they write, unless they're mighty filled with themselves. Mark Twain speaks

English high-toned as any American ought to, and writes dialogue more rustic than anyone I grew up with in the Mother Lode country. Old Jack London talks like a guttersnipe, which is only fair when you consider where he grew up, and uses such fancy words in his writing, it's a wonder he can spell 'em. You can't judge a book by its cover, or the author by his grammar. I've yet to meet your kinsman, Conan Doyle, but they say he talks more Irish than old Sherlock Holmes."

She grunted her way over a rock he didn't think she needed to be helped over before she said, "Sure and we're not after being related to thim Doyles with their lace-curtain ways. I think I follows your drift, now that I study on it."

He laughed. "You got your brogue down pat, but you're not too convincing talking cow. What have you got in these fool saddlebags? They weigh a ton."

"That's no doubt why I charmed you into carrying them for me," she said. "I didn't know how long we'd be on the trail. So don't be nosy about my feminine secrets. If you're very good, I may share some Bushmills I brought along for snakebite. I thought you said this damned canyon leads somewhere. How much higher can these damned old Rockies go?"

"Hell, we're well below timberline," he said. "Wait right here a spell, with that gun out, just in case. I want to see if someone shoots my head off when I stick it up over the rimrock."

She didn't argue. He left all but the Winchester with her and struggled up the last fifty yards, cursing and churning dust and gravel with his boots. When he hooked his elbow and the rifle over the last of the rock, he saw that he could see for miles and that they had the flat top to themselves after all. By the time he had Kathy and their gear topside, the sun was really fixing to go down behind the purple ridges to their west.

"Oh, how beautiful," she said, clapping her hands.

Stringer stared morosely at what he might have considered the beautiful sunset at other times. Then he gathered up his own load and growled, "Come on, if you're coming."

She stopped, gathered up her saddlebags, and draped them over her shoulder to hang down front and back as she skipped after him across the thin soil and slick rock in her high-buttons. "Roaming in the gloaming sounds better if one's not afraid of heights," she said. "How high are we right now, anyway?"

"Above sea level? Couple of miles, I reckon. But don't worry, you'll stop short by the time you fall two or three hundred feet."

She told him to remind her not to fall off the mesa, and asked where they were going when he headed inland through the scattered soap weed.

"I'm reminding you not to fall," he said. "The edge of this tabletop is jagged as hell. We have to work around some other clefts and canyons. I have to allow it's a lot easier in the daytime, though."

"Do you call this daylight?" she asked. "That sun's nearly down now."

He told her she ought to try it up here by moonlight. Then he said, "Keep it down to a roar. I'd like to let Kid Curry guess we're up here, and I have to poke about some for his particular canyon."

So they didn't speak for a time. Stringer was a mite turned around, not having been up here before with the low rays of the setting sun painting everything orange and purple. The moonlight he'd worked with last time had cast all the shadows the opposite way. But then he found the box

canyon he'd climbed out of, closer than he'd expected, and
dropped to his hands and knees to crawl the last few yards.

The infernal girl crawled right beside him. So they both
got to look over and down. "My God," Kathy gasped,
"you say you scaled those cliffs in the dark?"

"Not all of 'em," he said. "Just the one I had to climb.
Now hush and let me see if I can figure out what's down
there now."

It was hard to do that, for while the top of the mesa was
still sunlit, the depths of the box canyon were shaded deep
purple, and rocks were surprisingly hard to tell from anything more important in such tricky light. There were a lot
of rocks of all sizes and shapes scattered across the canyon
floor, most along the bases of the cliffs, of course, but
some out in the middle. There were no fires going down
there now.

"There, by that rock that looks sort of like a sea lion,"
Kathy murmured. "Isn't that a white sombrero?"

"More like a Stetson," he said. "But after that you got it
right. He's covering the mouth of the canyon from behind
that boulder."

He stared up the other way, where they'd had the horses
during his earlier visit. He counted four or five forms that
seemed too dark for boulders and shaped about right for
horses. When one of them moved, his eyes suddenly fo-
cused better. "I didn't think Kid Curry was a man who
inspired loyalty," he said. "There can't be more than a half
dozen or so of 'em left. Curry's so considerate that he's
posted one by the entrance in a sort of Arapaho stakeout
while the boss and the others get to fort up with their backs
to the back wall beyond the canyon creek."

"Oh, I see them now," Kathy said. "Isn't it surprising
how much easier it is to see a man behind a boulder when
you're way up here like this?"

"No. That's why I came up here. I wish we had a Bell telephone line to that posse outside. That old boy near the entrance would likely run back all the way to the others if he saw a determined rush coming his way. Once the posse riders made it up to the middle of the canyon where she widens out, they could just hunker down and lay siege until even Kid Curry has to figure out it's hopeless."

"Even I can see the fix they're in," she said, "and my paper refused to let me cover the war in Cuba. Just what do you want me to tell the posse, Stringer?"

"Forget it. You'd never make it all the way back to 'em before dark. I've got enough to worry about without having to picture you in that other canyon with a busted leg or worse."

She moved back, groped for her saddlebags, and opened one to produce a lady's purse. Then she opened that and got out a bitty makeup mirror, saying, "I told you I've been listening to those other boys spit and mutter. One of them said something about being in the Signal Corps during the war, and naturally I know Morse."

He stared blankly at her, then at the setting sun on the far side of the posse. "Thunderation! It might work!"

She replied demurely that there was only one way to find out. As she got to her feet, he followed her close to the edge of the mesa. When they looked down and out a piece, they could see the posse spread out along the nearest rise, dismounted, a lot better than anyone at ground level could have.

As Kathy raised her mirror, he said, "First let's see whether we're wasting our time or not. Signal that if anyone's picking up your gleaming dots and dashes he should fire his gun, once."

Kathy held the mirror higher to catch the half-sunk sun with it and experimented until she was bouncing orange light off the nearby edge of the rimrock. "I think I've got the sun in their eyes now," she said. "Let's see if I'm right."

She didn't have a shutter for her improvised heliograph, but by simply tilting it so the beam shot somewhere else, she was able to send dots and dashes, assuming she had the angle figured in the first place and that anyone was looking up this way in the second.

When one of the posse riders suddenly fired straight up, she laughed at the orange-and-purple smoke cloud above the posse. "You were saying, sir?"

Stringer grinned. "One guard only, posted just inside. Five or six others forted on the back slope, boxed. Say I'm fixing to do something about that one guard, but not to count on it. They can't answer. So what happens now is up to them."

He didn't wait for her to finish the message as he legged it back to the edge of the canyon, flopped down on his belly, and propped the Winchester over the edge and down. He could barely see that sea-lion-shaped rock, and could only guess if anyone was still behind it. He fired anyway, three times, and then someone down there was yelling, and judging by the sounds of crunching gravel, running pretty good as well. Then a rifle round spanged grit in his face as it hit just below him. He rolled back, spitting and cussing.

Kathy Doyle came over to him about the same time. "What was that all about? Those posse men are charging like infantry right now and—"

"Down!" he snapped as another rifle round hummed harmlessly over them from somewhere down below. She didn't take orders worth spit, and called him a brute when he swept her high-buttons out from under her with his boot and sat her on her bustle, if she'd been wearing a bustle.

"We can't see them in the dark half as well as they can

see us against the gloaming sky," he said. "Don't you ever do as you're told, Irish?"

"Not since I've been able to lick my old man. I want to see what's going on down there, damn it!"

He sat up and grabbed her as she started to rise. "Later. Once we've only got stars outlining our fool heads. I doubt either side can do much serious shooting down in that gloomy hole in the ground right now."

As if to make a liar out of him, the sound of rapid fire rose from the depths of the canyon. But when she struggled to get in on it, he shook her and insisted, "That's too much shooting for anyone to be aiming serious. You'll just catch a frustrated train robber's shot with your pretty face if you offer him any sensible target to shoot at right now." Then, because it was such a pretty face and because she kept struggling with him, Stringer kissed her and got a better grip on her at the same time.

Kathy kissed back, with as much enthusiasm as she showed about stealing stories from poor helpless male reporters. Then they had to come up for air, and she stared curiously at him in the soft sunset light. "Why did you do that?" she asked conversationally. "I didn't ride all this way to make love to a rival, damn it."

"I told you we'd share the story," he said. "There's enough news here for both our papers, and for once the papers will get it right. What happened at the O.K. Corral still depends on whether you study old clippings from the *Nugget* or the *Epitaph*. Neither paper had a reporter on the scene when whatever happened happened. This has to be a bigger fight than the one at the O.K. Corral, which never happened there, by the way. Stick with me, baby, and your byline may go down in history."

"All right. But let go of me. They don't seem to be

shooting down there anymore. Do you think it could already be over?"

He grimaced at the sunset, or its afterglow, now that the sun was really gone for good. "Not hardly," he told her. "What we just heard was the posse charging in and fanning out. I'll let you peek once it's darker. Meanwhile, take my word that Kid Curry and his boys are forted against the back walls of the box and that the posse riders have formed a siege line to keep 'em boxed. They'll have taken cover hither and yon at close but fairly safe rifle range, say one or two hundred yards."

"Why isn't anyone shooting, then?" she asked.

"It's dumb to shoot at targets you can't see. So this is where it gets tedious for a spell. Even when it's light again, it'll likely be a standoff until such time as Curry and his pals get desperate enough to go for broke or sensible enough to give up."

She wrinkled her pert nose. "Heavens, how long do you think we'll be stuck up here, then?"

"Depends on Curry's canteens and nerves. Overnight at least. That's why I brought my bedroll along."

"Oh," she said, and dug in her saddlebags some more as she added, "I like to think ahead too. I'd better get you drunk if I have to share a bedroll with you. That's all you're going to get from me, you know."

He said it was early yet. But he took the Bushmills with a nod of thanks, had a sip, and wheezed, "Smoooth." Then he put the fire out with canteen water.

She called him a sissy and took hers neat, muttering, "I might have known a Scotchman would ruin good whiskey with water."

He laughed. "Bite your tongue. The only time Cromwell was really skunked was when Highlanders from Lochaber and Irish troops from Ulster ganged up on him at Inverlochy."

He rolled over to the gear he'd dropped and began to unroll Tom the trader's bedding. "Highland and Irish rebels make a good team," he added, "if only you folk would get your Gaelic right. But those old stories were doubtless reported sloppy as well. I wonder if years from now anyone will know what really happened here, no matter how careful we report it. My rewrite editor is a pure fool for adding details that sound newsworthy, and if I leave anything out, he never asks me. He just makes one up to fit the blank space."

He spread the bedroll out on the firm surface. "Oh, Lord, I might have known such a fancy cuss would have lavender-scented sheets rolled up to go camping. They feel clean, at least. We won't get too stunk up with lavender if we keep our duds on, I reckon."

She moved over with her bottle to recline beside him on the softer but not that soft padding. "Anything has to be an improvement over those onions you've been eating," she said. "Where did you eat all those onions, anyway?"

He muttered he'd found some growing wild as he considered how old Tanya must have made out. He asked the gal with him at the moment if she knew of any other posses out after the train robbers.

She nodded. "Oodles. Some had left long before I could get up this way from Denver. The great train robbery has created quite a stir, you know."

He hadn't known. "The nickelodeon version was even greater," he said. "Those poor idiots down below didn't get enough money out of the deal to hire decent lawyers, and they're surely going to need some soon enough." He laughed and added, "I'll bet Sam Barca's going crazy right now. For if it's drawn national coverage, he'll have been sending wires all over creation, ordering me to cover it. Won't he be surprised when he gets my exclusive?"

She pouted and handed him the bottle. "I thought you said we were going to share the story, damn it."

He took a sip, noticed he didn't seem to need a chaser now, and after some study, decided, "I reckon there's no need to hold out on you. You had to be there to enjoy it. But I can give you the background material you need. You may as well get it right, seeing as how the infernal *Examiner* will surely run your feature on the front page no matter how you turn it in."

He brought her more or less up to date on his adventures with the Wild Bunch, leaving out some gossip about other ladies that would hardly be fit to print in any case. By the time he'd more or less finished, the first stars were out.

"I wish it was light enough to take notes," she said.

"Hell, it's not that complicated a story, Kathy. Man robs train. Posse catches up with man. All that's left is whether they give up or go down fighting. You'll be able to turn in an eyewitness report on that. Let your rewrite desk worry about the dates and details of Kid Curry's earlier trangressions if they need it for copy casting. It'll be in your paper's morgue."

"Pooh," she said, "you just said half such stuff is inaccurate, and you got to interview him in person about his wayward past."

Stringer shrugged. "Not enough to matter. He just said he wanted me to be his official biographer because, like I told you, he really wanted me to escape, earlier, and lead the law the wrong way."

"I can see why he's sore at you now," she said. "You'll no doubt get to be a sort of western legend now yourself, as the man who brought Kid Curry and the Wild Bunch to justice at last."

He sprayed both of them with Bushmills as she caught him with that as he was trying to drink some. "Not if I can help it, and please don't mention me in your own version, honey," he said. "I don't want to retire from the newspaper game the way poor old John Wesley Hardin ended his career."

She took the bottle back. "You sure drink sloppy. I've heard of that old gunslick. But I fear he was before my time with the *Examiner.*"

Stringer nodded. "I was just getting out of Stanford at the time. In his day, old John Wesley Hardin had made quite a rep. Then they salted him away for fifteen or sixteen years for blowing away a deputy sheriff. His rep outlasted his time in jail. So they'd barely let him out before as mean a cuss, who no doubt wanted to be as famous, shot old John in the back. The back of the ear, that is. Happened in El Paso in the summer of '95. Hardin was just minding his own business, shooting craps in the Acme Saloon. He never knew what hit him. That's why I don't want that kind of a rep. I'd sure hate to be shot from behind by some fool just out to get famous."

"I don't blame you," she said. "But did the man who shot John Wesley Hardin wind up famous?"

Stringer shrugged. "For a mighty short time. His name was Selman, and less than a year later a Deputy Scarborough killed him to win the same fame, until he in turn got blown away by...I'll be damned, Kid Curry! Small world, isn't it?"

"I'm going to die of an ague with all this booze on my bodice," she said. "But wait, if you got credit for the death or capture of Kid Curry, down there..."

He nodded. "That would make me the man who killed the man who killed the killer of John Wesley Hardin, the man who backed Wild Bill down. So, no thanks, I'd rather be remembered as a prissy newspaperman, if it's all the same with you."

She began to unbutton her bodice. "I won't tell if you won't tell, then," she said.

"Are we talking about Kid Curry's rep or your own?"

"We have to be practical," she said, "and it's already getting chilly up here. Turn your back and don't peek as I slip under the covers."

He turned away but rolled his eyes up at the stars. "Why me, Lord?" he asked, for he knew that while they'd both have at least their underthings on, this was shaping up to be a long night indeed. It was fair to make passes at reporters from rival papers, and so he had, more than once, back in Frisco. That's how he knew what a tease she was.

If she thought he was going to make a total fool of himself wrestling with her like that again, she had another think coming. She had the damned bottle in bed with her. So he sat cross-legged atop the blankets and proceeded to roll a smoke.

"My," she murmured, sleepily, "it must have been a longer day on the trail than I thought. These starched sheets sure feel heavenly. Aren't you coming to bed, Stringer?"

"Later, mayhaps," he growled. "It's early." Then he finished building his Bull Durham, lit it, and moved over to see what might be taking place down in the canyon.

Nothing was. Neither side had even built fires. He knew the men on both sides were crouched down there in the dark, tense as hell and no doubt bored at the same time. But bored or not, at least they all had enough worries to keep them awake and off the subject of women.

He finished his smoke and crawled back to the bedroll, hoping the pretty little thing had drunk herself to sleep, and that if so, she'd left some for him.

But when he rejoined her, Kathy said, "My paper's going to want some round numbers, at least. I'm sort of confused about that, Stringer. You said there was a really big gang down there, before, and now you say there's only a handful?"

He sat down on the blankets beside her again. "I could sure use some of that Bushmills now. I thought I explained that the Wild Bunch is really more like a wild bunch, lower-case, and that we, not they, consider it a formal organization with enlistment papers, rules, regulations, and so on. They're really no more than a mess of like-minded criminals, some petty and others as mean as hell. There must be over a hundred known outlaws the law has enrolled in what it calls the Wild Bunch, uppercase, at one time or another. But like their so-called Hole in the Wall, we're really talking about tumbleweeds. They come and they go, hiding out here there and everywhere, and the only mystery to that Hole in the Wall is why anyone would think owlhoots on the dodge would have a permanent address to begin with."

"They must have some way of getting together for big jobs, right?" she said.

"Sure they do. In real life it's called the Grapevine. They have no recognized leader. When one of 'em gets a grand notion to stick somebody up, he just lets all the shady landladies and barkeeps know about it, and as soon as enough of 'em look him up, they just go and do it. By this time more notorious Wild Bunchers like Butch Cassidy will have read about that train robbery in the papers. Whether they knew Kid Curry was planning it and didn't cotton to his plans, or whether they now feel left out and wistful, is anybody's guess. So-called members of the Wild Bunch have pulled jobs on their own from the Mex to Canadian border and from as far west as Oregon to as far east as Tennessee. I have it on good authority that Kid

Curry and Sundance were raiding a Texas house of ill repute for love toys while the law had them up in their so-called Hole in the Wall in the Green River headwaters. The reason Curry's boxed right now is that this time the law isn't searching for any outlaw kingdom. They've tracked a miserable handful of them to a poorly chosen hideout close to the scene of their last crime."

Kathy yawned. "Thanks to you, you mean. We were just riding around in circles until we ran into you, and Lord knows where all those other posses got lost. Come to bed, damn it. I'd really like to catch some sleep after all that riding."

He told her to go on and fall asleep if she wanted to. But she kept on insisting, and so he shucked his jacket, shirt, and boots to roll in with her, wearing just his jeans.

Then, as she welcomed him under the covers with open arms, he wondered why on earth he wanted his jeans on, for Kathy was stark naked as they met in a mutual warm embrace.

He thought it better to kiss her some more instead of commenting on her pleasant cure for insomnia. By the time she let him breathe some more, he was atop her, cradled by her responsive thighs and even sweeter flesh between them. So he thought it safe to say, "I thought you said you wanted to sleep sort of chaste, like that time on the coast train, honey."

"A whole damned night, without so much as a magazine to put myself to sleep with?" she said. "That time on the train down to Los Angeles was different. What kind of a girl checks into a Pullman berth with the whole world staring at her knowingly? Besides, as I told you at the time, I was being met at the station by another woman, and another woman always knows. Are you going to spend the whole night asking why I didn't want you to lay me that time, or would you like to lay me right, tonight, damn it?"

He did. He couldn't have laid still in such a grand position had he wanted to. By the time they were going at it nice and spunky, she was rolling her head from side to side, moaning and sobbing with real tears running down her cheeks. So he stopped what he was doing to her, kissed away some tears, and said, "I'm sorry, honey. I'm trying not to treat you rough, but there's not much padding, and I've wanted you this way so long and often—"

"Just do it, then!" she cut in, digging her nails into his back and wrapping her legs around his waist. "I've had this in mind since first we met," she sobbed, "and oh, honey, I'm so sorry about the times we've missed out on this that I can't help crying about it. I expected it to be marvelous, but the real thing feels so much better that I'm mad as hell at myself right now!"

CHAPTER
ELEVEN

It was no great surprise when guns started going off again by the cold gray light of dawn, even though it woke Stringer up with a start.

Then he noticed Kathy's head still lay nestled against his shoulder, and that although she was still half asleep, she seemed to be toying with his privates under the blankets. So that hadn't been the nicest wet dream he'd ever had, after all.

As he began to play with her in return, she yawned, murmured, "Faster, darling," then opened her eyes and said, "Oh, it's you. Let me wake up first and— Oh, what's that noise?"

"The boys down below must be early risers," he said. "Speaking of which, we ought to start thinking about getting dressed ourselves. For if that deputy sends a runner up here with any dumb messages—"

"We'll tell him all writers are bohemians," she cut in,

adding, "If you think I'm going to settle for just those two sweet fingers, now that you've gotten so fresh with them, you're just too prim and proper for the literary field."

He laughed, allowed he didn't want to be taken for a gent with no creative imagination, and they made love some more. He found it easy to bring her to climax ahead of him. He'd noticed earlier that she didn't try to hold back. But being a woman, and ergo more practical about sex than any man, once she'd had her wicked way with him, she murmured, "That was lovely. But I guess we have to get up before somebody comes, dear."

"I am up and I'm trying to come," he grunted. "Don't go icewater on me *now,* honey!"

She didn't. She began to move her hips skillfully as she told him, "Hurry. If you take much longer, I'll get hot again, and then where will we be?"

They decided it had to be heaven once he'd come and been told she'd murder him if he stopped now, for God's sake.

But all good things had to end, damn every one of them, and so they finally got dressed, polished off the last of the Bushmills and some canned pork and beans old Tom the trader had thought to travel with, and as the sun was just peeking over the higher ridges to the east, they crawled over to the canyon rim to see what all the noise might mean.

What it seemed, at first glance, was total confusion. Kid Curry and his pals were sending up the most gun smoke from their somewhat higher position against the back wall of the canyon. The posse riders were a lot easier to make out, since they lay or crouched among the rocks farther down, with their backs to Stringer and Kathy. From time to time a lawman would lob a round up at the train robber's smoke, then duck like hell before Kid Curry or one of his followers could return the compliment.

Kathy asked why they didn't help, and hoisted her skirts to get at her bitty .22. But Stringer told her not to be silly, explaining, "Those .22 shots would barely carry that far, and if they did, they wouldn't hurt a grown man."

"What about your rifle, then?" she asked.

"You sure are a bloodthirsty little gal," he said. "Those lawmen down there are wasting enough ammunition. Nobody would be forted behind a big rock in the first place if he didn't figure it would stop even a .44–40 slug. Like I said, it's a standoff. The owlhoots are acting the most unreasonable. So they must know they only have two ways to end it. They can die slow of thirst or lucky shooting, or they can surrender and die later, rope dancing."

She repressed a shudder. "I see a third way. If I was in a spot like that, I'd consider killing myself."

He shrugged. "Kid Curry told me, personal, that he considers that unmanly. He called a mad-dog killer called Tracy a sissy for shooting himself when there was just no other way out."

"In that case, how long do you expect this to last?" she asked.

"It's not for me to say. If that deputy in charge of the posse has any sense at all, he'll have sent riders to fetch extra water and, if possible, more gun hands. It's just a question of time. Neither side can get at the other without breaking cover, and that could be fatal at the range they're all pinned down at. I covered a couple of situations like this down in Cuba. They can drag on for hours or even days. But you said you wanted a bird's-eye view. I wonder if Waterloo looked this tedious, bird's eye. I know it doesn't in those paintings they've made of the battle since.

But considering how long it went on, they couldn't have all been shooting and charging like that all the time."

She pointed. "Look, there's that one with the white hat again, blasting away from that rock that sort of looks like a dead elephant."

Stringer nodded soberly. "I figured I missed him last night. If he keeps popping up like that, he's surely going to get hit, though."

Then the white hat fluttered up and away like a misshapen seagull, and he added, "See what I mean? They missed his scalp, however, and I see he's changed his position as well as his manners now."

She asked, "What if we were to sort of work our way along this rim until we were looking straight down at those killers, dear?"

He grimaced. "They might kill us. I know I'd shoot straight up at anyone looking straight down at me, and we're discussing no more than two hundred feet or so. That's point-blank with rifles. But lest you take me for a sissy who's afraid to pee on Kid Curry's hat, I've got two more, better reasons. As I said, it's a long way to fall, but nothing much to a bullet, and with the posse shooting so wild upslope, I'm not about to move into their line of fire."

She asked what his other reason might be.

"I explained about not wanting to get famous," he told her. "How could I hope to avoid that if I stood up here like a big-ass bird against the sky, shooting the one and original Kid Curry in the back?"

"That wouldn't be the same," she protested. "This is war."

But he shook his head. "That's not the way it would read in many a penny dreadful. I've always thought Pat Garrett took old Billy the Kid professional too. The Kid had, for God's sake, just shot two of Garrett's deputies in the back, and Garrett wasn't after him to kiss him. They met face to face in old Pete Maxwell's bedroom, both with their guns out, and the only crime anyone can lay on Garrett is that he fired first. He nailed the Kid through the heart, from the front, yet one fool writer after another keeps coming out with yarns about that no-doubt tensed-up lawman taking the Kid unfair. The poor old cuss even wrote his own book, declaring he'd done no such thing. But the myth of an invincible Robin Hood being slain by his best friend, dirty, still persists to haunt poor old Garrett. I expect to hear, any day now, about some otherwise forgettable cuss blowing Garrett away just so he can say he killed the man who killed Billy the Kid, Kid Antrim, Henry McCarthy, or whoever he was."

Kathy sighed. "Well, far be it for me to sully your reputation, you sweet old stud, but we'll soon be frying like eggs on this flat shadeless rock. We've got the story. Why don't we go on back down?"

He shot her a surprised look. "The story isn't over yet. Like I said, it could go on all day and even into the night. It all depends on how long their water and ammo holds out."

"Let me know when it's over, then," she said. "I'm going down to hunt for some shade. Are you sure you don't want to come too?"

He grinned at her. "Later."

She told him he was fresh and headed back across the mesa with her own lighter load. He watched her to make sure she didn't step in any serious cracks. Then she turned into a cute little dot, waved at him, and dropped from sight down that other canyon.

Stringer turned his attention back to the tedious gunfight in the canyon below. As the sun rose higher, he had to admit she had a point about fried eggs. It still surprised him she'd put comfort before being in at the actual kill, though. He knew she'd have little trouble writing it up as if she'd been there, once she was told about it. He was watching, and he was damned if he could come up with more than two possible endings. The most likely called for Curry and his pals to surrender. It was one thing to swear you'd never be taken alive, and another thing entire when you were tired, out of ammo, maybe hurt, and the law refused to shoot you anymore.

Stringer found himself typing the story he meant to hand in in his head. It was easy. All he needed was the final result. He'd use that as his lead-in and then tell his readers what had led up to it. He decided not to go into his own capture and his person-to-person interview with the late or recently captured and soon to be late Kid Curry. He'd get the names of the poor saps killed or captured with him from the posse, once they got around to doing either, damn them.

Stringer rose and moseyed over to the rim of the mesa to see if he could spot Kathy. Waving at pretty gals had to be more fun than staring down at rocks with gunslicks hiding behind them. The cliff he stood atop shaded the ground below well out across the scrubby infertile landscape. If she wanted shade at this time of the day, she could hunker down most anywheres.

Then he spotted her, sidesaddle, heading south alone.

"What the hell?" he muttered, then he sighed and said aloud, "Yep, the man who said perfidity's name was Woman must have met up with a gal like Kathy Doyle in his time."

He watched morosely as the pretty rival reporter topped a distant rise and vanished over it without even waving adios.

He hunkered down and began to roll a smoke as he

stared into the hole in the wall she'd chosen, musing aloud, "All right. You could likely beat me to the nearest telegraph office by at least a few minutes if I started after you this instant. Once you had the clerk's admiration, it would be first-come, first-served, and so there's just no way my story could beat yours to Frisco. But how in thunder are you planning to *end* it, you treacherous little thing?"

He lit his smoke and ambled back over to the canyon rim to see how they were doing. They weren't doing a thing different.

He lay back down, next to his Winchester, and mulled over all the pillow talk they'd enjoyed the night before during the interludes when they hadn't been enjoying one another.

"More fool me," he said aloud. "That'll teach me to tell a rival the odds are on capture. If she words it right, she just might get away with skipping the last details. She's got the robbery, likely knows better than me just how much was taken, and thanks to me, knows where the train robbers went and that the law caught up with 'em there."

He scowled down into the canyon and said, louder, "Damn you, Curry, if you go and give up now, I've been scooped by that sneaky gal again!"

He didn't want that to happen. So he grimaced, picked up the Winchester, and levered a round in the chamber to see what he could do about the pickle Kathy had left him in.

He bounced a round off the rock White Hat was hunkered behind. From his vantage point he could hit farther over the rocks, at least. Down below, a couple of the gents he wasn't aiming at looked up. The deputy in charge waved his hat as if he thought Stringer was doing something important and needed encouragement.

He didn't see that his modest efforts with one more gun

were making that much difference. But he must have worried the boys with Kid Curry some, for now they all seemed to be shooting up at him.

He rolled away from the rim as hot lead chewed up the rock for a spell. When he eased forward again, he chose a vantage point a little closer. He could tell at a glance that the posse riders had taken advantage of his distraction, for several of them had worked closer to the train robbers. Stringer decided one at least was too close when someone shot his hat off. But when the lawman crouched lower, ran his fingers through his hair and studied them, Stringer could see they hadn't split his skull enough to matter.

During a lull in the ragged fire, the deputy down there called out for Kid Curry to give it up, adding, "We got the water and ammo to last as long as it takes, Curry."

Kid Curry's reply was a snarl and a blaze of rapid fire from behind his own rock. Stringer gazed down to see what they might have done with poor little Opal's body. He spotted burned-out fires and wind-blown trash the length of the canyon, but nothing that had been alive down there the last time he'd inspected it by daylight.

Nothing but the horses, that was. The posse had naturally left their own mounts safe outside the canyon. But the mounts the owlhoots had come in with were still tethered near them, albeit off to one side and so far unharmed. Nobody in the posse had seen fit to shoot at a likely innocent horse, and of course, Kid Curry's bunch didn't want them hurt.

Stringer liked horses. On the other hand, he'd liked poor little Opal even more, and if those desperate bastards made any attempt at a bust-out, they'd have a hell of a time getting far on foot, even if one or more of 'em made it.

Stringer hesitated, snubbed out his smoke, and then, not

wanting to cause needless suffering, took careful aim and killed the nearest horse with a spine shot.

As it went down, spooking its tethered companions into a milling mass, a voice Stringer recognized as that of Kid Curry called out, "That's inhuman, you son of a bitch!"

So Stringer nodded, drew another careful bead, and put yet another pony in the dust. That and the screaming from all the owlhoots, now, inspired the remaining mounts to bust loose and tear off down the canyon. Stringer noted with approval that not one old cowhand in the posse was dumb enough to move until they'd run past him.

It took a spell to get sort of quiet again. Then the deputy called out, "I hope you see where that leaves you, old son. Why don't you just toss your guns out, and I can promise you a fair trial?"

Kid Curry fired in the direction of the older lawman's voice. "Try that for fair," he yelled, "you pony-murdering son of a Siwash whore and a wolverine! For I've rid high and I've rid low and I've never met such dirty fighters before in all my born days!"

The deputy called back, cheerfully, "Unlike your folk, mine was white, and married lawsome as well, you sweet-natured credit to the Indian Nation."

It worked. Kid Curry popped up from behind his rock to pump round after round in the deputy's general direction. The only reason he wasn't blown to shreds, in turn, was that he ducked back down before even Stringer could come unstuck. But as the men below him proceeded to chip away at his boulder with their own wild fire, Curry was moving to another one for shelter, and nobody but Stringer had as fine a view of his lizard crawl from one rock to the other.

Stringer fired almost without thinking. It was only when Curry yipped like a kicked dog and scrambled out of sight again that Stringer nodded grimly down through the drifting smoke to mutter, "That was for Opal, and it's not enough."

Then he had to move back to safety as they all started bouncing lead along the rimrock at once.

By the time they'd noticed he wasn't there anymore, or had to stop to reload, Stringer was peering down from another vantage point, with his hat set aside in hopes they might take his head against the bright sky as just another fool rock. The kitchen-match reek of gun smoke floated up to him, but nobody down in the canyon was firing anymore. They might have wanted to breathe.

Stringer couldn't make out any targets from his new position. They were hugging rock pretty tight down there. After a time he heard a less familiar voice call out, "Hey, Curry, are you all right?"

There was another lull. Then Kid Curry called back, "No. I'm hit. Could one of you boys get over here with some water?"

The one who'd asked, and now no doubt wished he hadn't, called back, "Not hardly. It's too far across open ground. Can you hold out until dark?"

"I reckon I'll have to," Curry replied. "I ain't bleeding too bad, but Jesus H. Christ, my mouth tastes dry."

Stringer was not, of course, the only enemy of the wounded outlaw with ears. But it still took him a few minutes to decide why the burly deputy had started a fire on the safe side of a big rock. Once he did, Stringer grinned down and muttered, "Oh, now that's just plain dirty."

It took the boxed owlhoots a lot longer. But within, say, half an hour, even Stringer could smell the ham they were frying and the coffee they were brewing. Once the whole canyon was reeking with the tempting odors, and Kid Curry had yelled some awful things about his mother again, the posse leader called back, "We'd be proud to share this with you boys, if only you'd toss them guns out first."

"Curry?" a plaintive voice called out.

"You go ahead and give up if you have to," their leader called back. "I'd just as soon die here than on the gallows like poor old Jack Ketchum. Why don't you go on down and coffee up with the sons of bitches so they can tear your fool head off with the rope?"

The hungry train robber didn't throw his gun out. He rose just high enough to aim it down the canyon as he sobbed, "You no-good torturing fiends!"

Then Stringer and a couple of posse riders peppered his rock and he dropped back down. "Hey, Curry," he yelled. "They're closing in on us as well as torturing us."

"I see the one with the red bandana," Curry called back. "Hold your fire until you see him better. We got to make our ammo last. Do you reckon you could at least toss me a bandolier without exposing yourself?"

Some unseen helper threw the loose ammo belt like a dead snake, and it landed almost close enough to the boulder Kid Curry was hunkered behind. But almost wasn't good enough when Stringer blew it back out of reach with his second try. Kid Curry called out to his followers, "Get that son of a bitch up there on the rimrocks before he pisses on my damned old hat!"

Another voice called back, "We've been trying to. He keeps moving about and only shows a mighty small portion of himself when he shoots back."

"Who's up there, Charlie Siringo?" Curry called up. "I know Joe Lefors don't shoot that good, and somebody mighty good at tracking has to be the author of our woes."

"I don't call myself an author," Stringer called back, cheerfully enough. "Writer is good enough for a man who works at it more regular."

There was a moment of silence. Then Kid Curry called back, "I might have known it was you, Stringer. We should have killed you, or just left you on that damned old train."

"I won't give you any argument about that," Stringer yelled. "What did you boys do with the body of the gal who fell down the cliff the other night?"

Kid Curry snorted in disgust. "We buried her, of course. What did you expect us to do, stuff her?"

"I'd be obliged if you'd tell me where, Curry."

"I know you would. That's why I don't aim to tell you."

Stringer resisted the impulse to fire at the taunting voice. It made more sense to fire at targets one could see, and the gruff old deputy down below was even taunting Stringer now with the smell of all that cooking.

Stringer moved back to the bedroll, rummaged out a can of tomatoes, and found it helped some. Then he had a nastier idea and took a can of Arbuckle Tom the trader had been traveling with. Arbuckle was made in Frisco and widely admired in cow camps as a brand of coffee it was just about impossible to make wrong if you had any fire and water at all to work with.

He didn't. "I got something for you old boys," he called out. "I sure hope you can reach it." Then he threw the can.

It landed just his side of their rock screen, as he'd aimed it to. The can burst open on the rocks to scatter ground coffee in every direction. Even one of the closer-in posse riders sort of sobbed when he saw all that good stuff going to waste. Kid Curry went sort of crazy. "Now that was just about as nasty as nasty can get!" he yelled, and rose high enough for Stringer to draw a bead on him with the Winchester. As he fired and the already wounded outlaw leader dropped out of sight again, the whole posse cheered. But Stringer wasn't so sure, and sure enough, when one of his followers called out to him, the surly Kid Curry called back, "Just a graze, but no shit, this is starting to add up. Can't you at least try to toss me my damned old canteen?"

Stringer was ready when someone tried. The canteen landed closer to Curry's rock than the ammo belt had. But as he saw a booted foot reach out to see if it could hook the canteen's strap, Stringer fired and blew the canteen apart. Then he swore at himself for not thinking fast enough to aim at Curry's foot.

But the boxed owlhoots found the results of his shooting painful enough, judging from their cussing and wild gunfire. The posse was cheering and jeering as they watched the contents of the shot-up canteen paint a chocolate-brown streak down the slope toward them. When things calmed down some, the deputy in charge called out, cheerfully, "Don't let that upset you, boys. There's plenty of water, running, down this way. Throw away your hardware and you can drink till you bust, for all I care."

Stringer chuckled dryly at the picture, recalling the nasty little rill farther down the canyon. It was no doubt running clearer now that all the whores and hangers-on had lit out. But it would take a spell indeed before it was fit for human consumption.

But a pony could probably use it, and that thought reenforced the guilt he was beginning to feel about a chore he'd been sort of putting off since sunrise.

Horses needed a lot more water than humankind. A mustang running free could get by on one awesome swilling a day. But brutes being worked had to be watered three times as often, not because they were sissies, but because they sweat more and couldn't carry anyone if they swilled a day's ration all at once. The chestnut gelding he'd been riding had been resting all this time in a cool canyon, but by now it had to be mighty thirsty. Stringer knew better than to hope his pretty but sneaky rival, Kathy, had watered his mount in passing. But like someone reading a good book and needing to take a leak at the same time, he'd been putting the chore off a page at a time in hopes the saga of Kid Curry might be resolved any minute. For there was more to the chore than simply dropping over the rim and running down to spill canteen water in the chestnut's nose bag. They only had about half a canteen between them now. It was enough to carry Stringer through the day, but hardly a healthy swallow for a thirsty pony.

He stared down into the box canyon for a few more minutes to see that nothing important seemed to be going on. How long the train robbers could hold out depended on how much ammo, water, and guts they had up behind those rocks. Stringer knew he'd have to be mighty discouraged to surrender for a hanging if he was in their boots. So, like it or not, he just had to see to his mount.

From the way the chestnut nickered to him as he was sliding down the last of the rocks choking the other canyon, Stringer knew he'd been right about the poor brute suffering from thirst. He untethered it, patted its muzzle, and soothed, "Come on. We'll get you to that other canyon's water soon enough."

It took longer than that, leading the pony along the base of the cliffs in the shade of the rimrock. It was fighting to bust free and go dowsing for water on its own by the time they got around a rocky bend to spy the posse ponies loafing in the same shade near the canyon mouth. The two young hands who'd been stuck with wrangling for the rest of the posse asked Stringer if he knew what was going on up the canyon. He told 'em it was a Mexican standoff, so far.

"Jesus," one said, "once they last past noon, we'll be baking like beans here, under the durned old sun ball!"

Stringer led his own mount closer to the canyon mouth

and risked a look-see up the canyon. "No you won't," he said. "The only ones likely to shoot at you are up at the far end, around more than one bend. Come noon you may be able to still find some shade a few yards up."

Then he led his pony in a ways. The meager canyon stream soaked into the gravel without escaping from the canyon, a point Kid Curry had no doubt noticed when he'd found the hideout. But by kicking some with his boot heel, Stringer was able to hollow out a little puddle pool where water still ran. The chestnut lowered its muzzle and proceeded to drink with so much pure pleasure, it might have gotten a hard-on if it hadn't been a gelding. Stringer stood by, then hauled its head up and told it, "That's enough, you fool sponge. I'm going to leave you out yonder with the other ponies now. Those kids look kind enough to prevent you dying of thirst, and I'm sorry I treated you so mean just now."

He led it out and left it in charge of the wranglers, saying, "I'm going up a ways for a look-see. My features editor might want some comments from the posse riders and a few lines about what this fight looked like from ground level."

He saw they didn't know what he was talking about, albeit neither was impolite enough to say so, and headed back into and up the canyon.

He couldn't work his way too far before the situation began to get thoughtful. The posse riders hunkered behind rocks a hundred yards or more ahead of him had moved up that far under cover of darkness. Stringer leaned his Winchester against a rock out of Kid Curry's rifle range and commenced to roll a smoke. Even if he managed to make it to the skirmish line, he could see from where he stood that the gang was screened a lot better from down here. He'd have never been able to put that round in Curry from anywhere down here. He wasn't looking forward to climbing back up alone. Maybe, after he'd smoked on it, he'd talk some of the others into following him topside so they could all give the gang a good dusting. How anyone was to come and join him without exposing his back to owlhoot fire was the thing to study on the most. The advantage of a higher field of fire hardly balanced the disadvantage of risking a rifle round in the back.

Stringer had barely gotten his Bull Durham going when they all saw a flash of white against the back wall of the canyon. Stringer thought, at first, it was that one with the white hat trying to make the posse waste ammo. If he was, he was waving his hat around too much for anyone to think it had a head attached to it. That was likely why nobody on Stringer's side fired.

Stringer realized it had to be a white kerchief when the burly deputy, much closer to it, called out, "All right, old son, we see your parley signal. What do you want?"

"Terms," the train robber waving the kerchief called back. "If I lay down my arms, do I have your word I won't get strung up on the nearest tree?"

"Sure you do," the deputy called back. "Whether a judge and jury decides to hang you more formal ain't for us to say. But hell, your trial will surely take longer than you boys have behind them fool rocks."

"Look, I ain't wanted for anything worse than robbery," the desperado replied in a worried whine. "Do you reckon there's a chance I'll get off with Life at Hard?"

"Quien sabe?" the deputy informed him. "You might even be out in twenty years. I wouldn't like that either. But you have my word I mean to stomp all you piss ants dead if you make us wait till dark, whether you get any of us as we charge in or not."

There was a moment of silence. Then they heard another voice call out, softer, "How about it, Curry? Anyone can see how hopeless this is getting."

From behind his own rock Kid Curry called back, "You boys do as you've a mind to. I mean to end it here."

There was a longer silence as the others consulted and no doubt argued about it some. Then the one who'd been signaling cried out, almost sobbing, "Hold your fire. We're coming out."

The posse did as a considerable hardware collection got lobbed their way over the rocks. Then the pathetic remains of the Wild Bunch—or this chapter of it, at least—rose with hands in the air to move down the slope into the waiting arms of the posse.

Then another shot rang out and everybody froze. But since they saw Kid Curry had gunned neither a posse rider nor one of his surrendering sidekicks, they moved down some more.

"What was that all about, Curry?" the posse leader called out. When nobody answered, he decided, "One of you rascals had best go see if he's still with us."

The train robber closest to Kid Curry's final hideout shook his head. "Not this child. He's been feeling poorly, and his temper can be uncertain even when he feels good."

The posse leader cocked his gun. "Do as I say. I'm appointing you because me and mine are even more uncertain about the son of a bitch."

The man he'd picked moaned, "Oh, Lord, why does it always have to be me?" Then he turned to move back up with his hands still high. "Don't do it, Boss," he called out. "I'm coming in neighborly and unarmed, against my will, see?"

Then he got to the place where Kid Curry lay, gasped in either dismay or sheer relief, and called out, "He's dead! He just now blowed his own brains out!"

So Stringer, having farthest to walk, was about the last one there as Kid Curry's friends and foes alike gathered round to pay him their last respects.

The run-to-earth young killer lay sprawled on the scree like a discarded rag dolly, his six-gun still gripped in his gun-smoke-grimed right fist. His face could have been said to be wearing an expression of sweet repose if it hadn't been so blackened with smoke and if there'd been more left to his skull. There were gobbets of blood and brains spattered all over the dry rocks.

The deputy caught Stringer's eye. "Well, thanks to you," he said, "that's the end of the dangerous rascal, and I sure wish he'd done the world that favor sooner."

One of the dead man's erstwhile comrades gulped and muttered, "Whoever would have thought he'd do a thing like that? I mind him sneering like anything when we got word Harry Tracy had killed himself, and he always said Johnny Ringo was a sissy Jew boy for doing the same, down Arizona way."

Stringer shrugged. "Well, empathy was never his strong point, you know." When even the deputy didn't seem to know the meaning of the word, Stringer explained, "Empathy is the ability to picture yourself in another person's boots."

"Hell, I can do that," the deputy said, "even if I can't spell it."

Stringer nodded. "Most of us can, to some extent. I suspect that's what separates the halfway decent from the total bad. That poor mad dog at our feet never tried to understand even his fellow outlaws. He just lived from day to day, and when the time came for him to find himself in Harry Tracy's or Johnny Ringo's boots, he just forgot what he'd said about 'em and did what he felt like doing."

"I hope someone has an old tarp they won't need after

we wrap this mess up to tote to town," the deputy said. "I never heard before that Johnny Ringo was Jewish. Do you reckon he was?"

"His real name was Jacob Rhinegold," Stringer said. "After that your guess is as good as mine, and since all three of the murderous rascals were nice enough to kill themselves, who cares?"

CHAPTER
TWELVE

Stringer parted company with the joyous posse and their sad-faced prisoners when, near the railroad line, someone said a fork in the trail led to the nearest jerkwater but that they were fixing to take their prisoners and what was left of Kid Curry on to the county seat. Stringer wasn't sorry to see the last of them. He didn't like to fib, and more than one old boy had asked if he had any notion who'd winged Kid Curry and encouraged him to end the standoff so early in the day. Since more than one of the younger and dumber riders were sure they'd gotten off at least a few rounds at the rascal, Stringer felt his reputation might still be safe.

It was late afternoon when he parted company with some pines as well, to spy a water tower and some sun-silvered frame structures ahead. He rode into town and tied up near the Western Union sign he'd spotted. He wasn't too surprised to note the sidesaddle on another mount hitched in front of the telegraph office. As he was going up the steps, Kathy Doyle came out the door, looking as if butter wouldn't melt in her mouth. Stringer nodded at her and said, "What kept you? You had at least two hours lead on us."

"I got lost in the woods for a time," she said, "and then, of course, I had to take a bath at my hotel just up the street. I took the liberty of checking us in as Mr. and Mrs. Jones. How did it go out there, darling?"

He smiled at her incredulously. "They gave up. How come you had to leave so early?"

She met his eyes boldly as ever as she replied, demurely, "To tell the truth I had, ah, feminine hygiene to attend to, and you'd just told me how it was sure to turn out."

"Me and my big mouth. You've already wired your own scoop in, of course?"

"How could I?" she answered innocently. "I had to wait for you here so we could share the story, remember?"

He chuckled fondly down at her. "You're really something. You were just now wiring home for money, right?"

"As a matter of fact," she said, "I just alerted the city desk to stand by for front-page news I hoped to hand in by later this evening. Surely you don't think I'd betray your trust after all we've, ah, been to one another, dear?"

"The thought might have crossed my mind. How do you reckon to prove you didn't just scoop me again, Kathy?"

She dimpled up at him. "Easy. I haven't even written my version of recent events. There was no way I could until I was sure how things turned out. I'm not allowed to *guess* about such details, you know." She saw he was still unconvinced, and added, "Look, why don't you go in and wire your feature now? When you're done, you'll find me at the Drover's Rest near the depot, room 203, working on my own."

He frowned at her uncertainly. "How come?" he asked. "Why are you so anxious to let me scoop you?"

She fluttered her lashes. "I'll tell you just what I want you to do to me when we're alone at the hotel. If you must know, our evening edition is going to press right now out on the coast. There's no way they can run anything I send before the morning edition. That gives me plenty of time, and if you'd like to fill me in some more, at the hotel, I might pay you back with a French lesson."

"Well, I see I may have misjudged you after all, and filling you in is sure fun," he said. "I hope you understand I can still make the *Sun*'s last edition if I get cracking. We go to press later than the *Examiner*. That's likely how we scoop you so often."

She shrugged fatalistically. "That's not my fault. I only work for the *Examiner*. I don't run it. At least we'll both be on the front page tomorrow morning."

He nodded. "Room 203. Got it," he said, and moved past her to enter the telegraph office.

"Oh, I almost forgot," she said, following. "I meant to wire my landlady I'd be coming back to Frisco soon. Would you mind, terribly, if I dropped her a teeny-weeny warning to have my quarters ready for me, or us, if you're headed that way, dear?"

"Go ahead," he said. "I have to compose one mighty long wire in any case."

So they each found space along the stand-up writing table inside the door, and sure enough, Kathy had scribbled a short message and asked the clerk behind the counter to send it before he could finish the first page, fast as he'd learned to block letter in the field. She rejoined him, gave him a friendly peck on the cheek, and murmured, "Hurry, I can hardly wait." And then she was gone.

It made it easier for him to write his story. He knew

Sam Barca would dig plenty of background material from the morgue to flesh out the feature, so he didn't bother with dates and details of past misdeeds by the Wild Bunch. Everyone had lots of stuff on them on file. It was their own fault for acting so wild. Stringer concentrated on the last seventy-two hours or so of Kid Curry's desperate life; the forty-eight hours it had taken the posse to track the train robbers down, skipping his own part in the process; and the overnight siege in the canyon, leaving his own marksmanship out of that as well. He consulted the field notes he'd taken, riding with the posse, to make sure he correctly spelled all their names and the names of the less notorious surviving train robbers. He played up the suicide, since that seemed such an example for the youth of these United States, and managed to get it all on five pages of night-letter forms. Then he took his feature to the clerk and said, "I know I wrote all this on night-letter paper. But I want it sent straight, collect, at day rates."

The Western Union man scanned the neatly penciled message and whistled softly. "At a nickel a word, this is going to cost your paper a pretty penny. But I suppose you and that lady reporter who was just in here know what you're doing."

As he started to turn away Stringer asked, in a desperately casual tone, "Did she send as many pages as me just now?"

The clerk shook his head. "Not just now. Earlier. You have to ask her what she sent and about all the wires from Frisco she's been getting all evening. I'm not allowed, even though I know you two are pals."

Stringer nodded. "That's all right. I've a pretty good idea what she sent earlier. Like you said, we're pals."

Then he went out, led the chestnut to a nearby livery,

and asked the young hostler on duty if he knew Tanya Dillinger from the S Bar Diamond.

"I know the lady to howdy," the youth said. "She comes to town now and again, why?"

"This chestnut and all its gear belongs to her. How much will it cost me to board it here until she comes to town again?"

"We ask two bits a day," the young hostler replied. "But I don't know when we'll see her, next."

Stringer added in his head, dug out a five-dollar silver note, and handed it over. "This ought to last as long as it takes even a placid woman to get weary with her four walls. When next you see her ride by, give her a yell. She might not know she owns this pony. I'd best leave her a note in a saddlebag explaining the situation."

The youth allowed that few women could stay away from the shops in town more than two weeks at a time in decent riding weather. Stringer kept his message neither cold nor mushy. He wanted the big blonde to remember him as he'd always remember her, as a pal.

Then, having shed his excess baggage in a sensible way, Stringer went to the Drover's Rest to see how his other old pal was doing. He found her up in 203, editing yellow Western Union paper on her dressing table. She was sitting at it naked, save for her silk stockings and high-buttons. As she leaped up to greet him with an enthusiastic kiss, he said, "I'm glad you're half dressed. There's a westbound flyer stopping here for water in less than an hour. If you're heading back out to the coast with me, you'd best put a mite more on, though."

She moved over to the bed and flopped down the same way that gal on the second landing liked to pose for him. "I'm looking forward to riding all the way home with you," she purred, "but if we have a whole hour to kill . . ."

He sighed. "You know damn well we'd surely miss that train, once we got started, for time flies and other chores just don't seem to matter, once you're in bed with someone pretty. Are you sure you're not out to make me miss that train, Irish?"

She looked hurt. "Heaven forfend! I said I was looking forward to your riding with me all the way back to Frisco."

"Bueno," he said. "Get some duds on and we may have time for supper here, after we send your own version of that canyon fight."

She agreed and got back up to start dressing as he sat down at her dressing table to read what she'd written so far. She asked what he thought of her writing, and he said she was good, which was fair, since she'd sure made up a lot of stuff. None of her colorful wild west crap could be checked out by anyone who might matter. At this late date few members of the actual posse would be able to say, for sure, who'd said what to whom, so dramatic, as they brandished their piratical weapons. That's what she called six-guns—piratical weapons.

"I notice you've yet to finish this, Kathy," he said. "You sort of left the end open for grabs."

She began to button her bodice. "I had to know how it ended up in that canyon before I could end it on paper, dear. What time did they finally surrender?"

"Hour or so after you lit out," he said. "Make it anytime before noon and nobody will deny it. Want me to write a few lines about the last dramatic speeches?"

"I'd better do that, dear. You tend to write just a little tersely for my readers."

He was too polite to point out a news item didn't have to be filled with florid phrases when it was at all interesting, or true.

When she'd finished dressing and asked where they'd

have supper, Stringer said, "There's a place near the depot that looks clean, at least. Don't you want to take this story with you to turn in, honey?"

She twinkled. "Oh, how clumsy of me." Then, as she took them from him to put in her purse, she smiled sort of dirty and added, "I see what you mean about lovemaking being distracting. Just thinking about us aboard that train almost made me forget my first draft."

"How in thunder can you send in a first draft by wire," Stringer asked as they left, "speaking of which—"

"I always go over my work a time or two," she cut in. "I told you there's no way for me to make the final edition today, darling. I thought I'd rework it on the train, before it gets late enough to ask the porter to make up our berth, of course, and maybe send it in from Salt Lake, Elko, maybe Reno. We'll be stopping at all those places, won't we?"

"Salt Lake before midnight," he said. "After that you'll look silly getting off and on in your nightgown."

She laughed, asked him who said she'd planned on spending the coming night in any nightgown, and took his arm. So he took her to supper. He had plenty of spending money right now.

Kathy waited until they were having more coffee with their desserts before she asked him, thoughtfully, if something was upsetting him.

Stringer smiled and looked around. "No, I like this place fine. I always wanted stuffed animal heads on my walls when I was little."

"I thought you might be brooding about something," she said. "You don't seem quite as, well, eager as you did last night atop the mesa. Have you started to take me for granted, this soon?"

"Kathy," he said, "if there's one thing no man ought to

do with you, taking you for granted has to be it. Finish your pie, or let me if you don't want it. We still have to get our tickets and check your carpet bag."

She shook her head and told him she always kept the bag on the floor between them with her.

"Let's go see about those tickets, anyway," he said. "I sure don't want to miss that train."

They didn't. Kathy was tapping a pretty foot on the station platform by the time the westbound came in, hissed steam all over them, and let them aboard.

Since she'd said something about reworking her story, and since they kept the liquor back there in any case, Stringer made sure of their berth with the conductor. Once their tickets had been punched, he led Kathy back there. He noticed she still made him tote her small but compactly packed bag.

By this time the locomotive had swallowed enough water and the train was moving again. They found a table near the exit to the rear platform and moved to the bar to order them some drinks. As he moved both ways, he couldn't help noticing a sultry-looking gal in a maroon velvet outfit, seated alone at her own table and not too pleased about that, if he was reading her lonesome eyes at all correctly.

That was the trouble with women, he told himself, getting the drinks unspilled to the table Kathy was at. Women seemed to come into a man's life like rain. They either left you parched or poured more than you could absorb at once, and of course, if you tried to juggle two at once, you were likely to wind up with none at all again.

He sat down facing Kathy with his back to the lonesome gal. It helped some. But her perfume sure smelled nice. He slid Kathy's glass across to her, saying, "I see you haven't started your rewrite yet."

"I think you may be right about second drafts being a waste of time," she said. "I'll just add a paragraph about those bandits coming out with . . . their hands up?"

He nodded. "Yep. That's usually required by the law."

So she sipped her drink and said, "I can fill that in when we get to Salt Lake. When do you suppose they'll want to make up the berths, darling?"

Stringer felt very aware of the mystery woman behind him as he mumbled, "Nine-thirty or so. I wonder if I'll have time to check out that lead about Pearl Hart when we stop for water at Grand Junction."

She perked up. "Could the notorious Pearl Hart be at Grand Junction, dear?"

"I don't know," he said. "She just got out of prison and she has to be someplace. Old Sam Barca's been after me to do a feature on her. But nobody seems to know for sure where she is these days. They say she'd changed her appearance as well as her manners since being sent up for robbing the Globe stage back in '98. She just got out early for good behavior, no doubt feeling older and wiser. Old Joe Booth, the good-looking owlhoot who tempted her down the primrose path, is still in prison and likely to stay there. It was far from the first such stunt he'd pulled."

Kathy made a wry face. "I recall the case and the pictures published of her at the time. I don't know why you men consider bandit queens so glamorous. To me she just looked dumb and pathetic in that man's attire they posed her in with all those no-doubt empty guns."

"Well," Stringer said, "I have to allow Belle Starr was ugly as sin. But judging from her pictures, old Pearl Hart wasn't too bad-looking. Bitty round face, sort of plain with no makeup and all. But anyone could see she had a cute little shape under those oversized cowboy duds. Anyway, the last Sam heard, she was on the lecture circuit with

Frank James, Cole Younger, and other older and wiser re-
formed outlaws, lecturing on the evils of demon rum and
wild wild women, or in old Pearl's case, likely wild wild
men. She was brought up honest enough in Canada.
Eloped with a gent named Hart, and when he couldn't support her in the Arizona mining country, she left him to take
up with men with more money and maybe less sense. Sam
Barca thinks she'd make a good feature, now that she's
said to be more refined. I don't mean to call her any bandit
queen when I catch up with her. It wouldn't be fair to call a
poor young gal who went wrong a dumb thing like that.
Lord knows how Sam will edit it, of course, and maybe
she'd like to be called a bandit queen. It might sell more
tickets to her temperance lectures."

Kathy sipped some more and asked, "What makes you
think she could be in Grand Junction, darling?"

"If I knew she was," Stringer answered, "I'd have to get
off there, Pullman berth or not. But like I said, it's just a
lead. She's been touring this part of the country of late, and
Barca says there's a theatrical booking agent in Grand
Junction who might know where she's appeared so far, and
more important, where she may be going next. I dunno,
though. This train only stops there a few moments to take
on boiler water. I doubt there's time, and like you said, she
may be stale news now. They don't run stages out of Globe
anymore."

Kathy looked thoughtfully down at her glass and mused
half to herself, "They hardly run stagecoaches anywhere
now. Wouldn't that make Pearl Hart the last stagecoach
robber who ever lived?"

Stringer shrugged. "Unless someone else robs another,
soon. I got to thinking about those new horseless carriages
as I was leading a horse to water this morning. At first
glance those odd contraptions make little sense. They can't

go lots of places a pony could get you. But on the other hand, when you don't have anyplace to go, you don't have to oat and water 'em at least twice a day. You can let the fool machine just sit for a month or more and then just climb aboard and ride off with it. That'd be mighty handy for say a city cuss who only takes his wife and kids for a buggy ride on weekends, right?"

She frowned across the table at him. "What in the world could horseless carriages have to do with stagecoach hold-ups, dear?"

"Putting coaches out of business, of course," he said. "The only coaches still in service are working the back roads between rail lines. Mark my words—in just a few years they'll have motor coaches going too fast for road gents to rob, easy, that is."

Kathy said, "Hmm, as I said, that makes her the last of the old-time road agents, and I see a woman's angle as well. Just what does this amazing woman look like, honey?"

"I haven't seen any recent pictures of her. She'd be thirty or so now, with a handsome figure and let's hope more in the way of eyebrows. They say she's either darkened her hair or let it grow natural to look more like the rest of you Gibson Girls."

Kathy had that hunting look in her eyes now. But she was trying to hide it as she finished her drink. "I'll just tighten my story up and maybe wire it from Grand Junction. Why don't you give me the name of that booking agent, and even if we don't have time to see him, we might be able to wire him for the information when we stop at Salt Lake, see?"

He frowned thoughtfully, then brightened. "Lord love you if you don't think circles around us poor brutes. Your notion works. If he's in the city directory at Grand Junction, we can compose as long a message to him as we want, riding on to Salt Lake, and if he answers us by night letters, we can have him send to us in Frisco—"

"You're willing to share the feature with me, then?" she cut in.

"Sure," Stringer said. "You'd share fair and square with me, wouldn't you?"

She said she sure would. So he wrote the booking agent's name on the edge of her manuscript as she hauled it out, but told her, "All I have is the name. If I can't find him listed in the directory at the depot when we stop—"

"Leave it to me," she said. "If he does any business at all, they'll know him at the Western Union, and I have to go there in any case."

So he agreed, picked up their empty glasses, and headed back to the bar for refills. He found the sultry gal in the maroon outfit standing there to get her own glass refilled. As he waited for his own order, she sort of purred, "I couldn't help overhearing some of the conversation you've been having with that sweet young thing. I take it you're both newspaper writers?"

He nodded. "Yes, ma'am, albeit for rival papers."

She blinked at him incredulously. "You don't *look* that stupid. I hope you have some good reason for giving a rival reporter a tip like that. I know she's pretty, and I couldn't help hearing those remarks about berths later, but are you sure you can trust anyone that far?"

He smiled at her. "About as far as I could throw this club car, one-handed. But we'll see how things work out, once we get to Grand Junction. Will you still be here, ma'am?"

She said she wouldn't miss it for the world. So he took his order back to the table to find Kathy busy as all get out with her reworking of the Kid Curry feature. He could see she didn't want to talk right now. It might have seemed impolite for him to start up with the gal at the next table, so he found a magazine in a rack across the way and read about the Irish Question for a spell. The British government sure seemed more confused about the Irish Question than any Irish folk he'd met so far.

It took that magazine and another before someone yelled out, "Grand Junction, next stop!"

Kathy hastily scooped up her homework to shove in her carpet bag, saying, "I'll go forward and ask how much time we'll have here."

When he offered to go along and at least tote her bag, she was off and running before he could get up. He settled back with a sigh, rolled a smoke, and then, as he'd expected, they were moving again.

The sultry gal at the next table observed, "From that smug expression you're wearing, now one might assume you wanted to ditch that young lady back there."

"I never ditch ladies, ma'am," he said. "But to tell the truth, I sort of figured she might ditch herself."

"Why? She wasn't bad-looking, and you have booked a double berth, haven't you?"

"The evening's still young. Since you've been such a good sport, despite your curious nature, I'll tell you what's going on. But wouldn't you like me to fetch us both more drinks first?"

She said she liked both suggestions. When he rejoined her at her table with their refills, he explained, "Miss Kathy Doyle, as you surmised, is a mighty sneaky little thing. Earlier today she beat me to town in order to scoop me on the capture of some train robbers. She sent all but the ending, which she didn't know. Then, when I showed up so's she could ask me how it had all turned out, she sent a shorter coded message, telling her own editor to use one of the two endings she'd submitted earlier. I'd already told her I figured the bandits would be taken alive. So when I told her they had, she wired home just before she let me put my own story on the wire, see?"

The older but not bad-looking brunette shook her head. "No, I don't. How could you be so nice to her just now, knowing she'd beaten you like that?"

"Easy," he said. "She didn't. Our stories will hit the stands about the same time. She was fibbing about her own paper's night edition. Her story, for the *Examiner,* will say the train robbers, including the notorious Kid Curry, were taken alive. My story will say, more truthfully, that Kid Curry refused to surrender and committed suicide."

The gal in maroon gaped at him, then laughed as she got the whole picture. "You outfoxed a real vixen, who's going to have a time explaining *that* news item! But what was all that nonsense about bandit queens supposed to accomplish?"

"Letting her hang herself higher. Had she dealt halfway honest just now, I'd have relented and let her wire in the right version at Salt Lake, seeing as I'd still go to press a little ahead of her paper. But as you just saw, there's not an ethical bone in her otherwise handsome figure. The name I gave her was real enough. I talked with that booking agent a few days ago and he told me he had no idea where I might find Miss Hart. He'll tell Kathy the same thing. But a night in Grand Junction sniffing red herrings won't hurt her, and whether you believe it or not, there's a limit to my good humor. I wasn't looking forward to kissing that treacherous little gal all the way to Frisco."

She was beaming at him in open admiration now.

"By the way," he said, "my handle is Stuart MacKail, and I'd rather be called Stringer, Miss . . .?"

"Hart, Pearl Hart," she replied demurely.

He raised a doubting eyebrow, having met other strangers in the night who'd tried to have fun at his expense. Then he slowly nodded. "You look better now that you've lost some of that baby fat and put some eyebrows on. I can see why you found our conversation so amusing. Do I have to look for you some more or do you feel up to granting me that interview my editor wants? I promise I'll try to make you look good in my wild west feature."

The notorious Pearl Hart smiled sort of dreamy-eyed at him. "We'll have plenty of time to talk between here and Frisco. I've got a private compartment up forward, and to make no bones about it, I just got out of prison and you're about the best-looking young stud I've run into since they let me out!"

So in the end Stringer wound up with two grand scoops as well as the pocket money he'd picked up here and there along the owlhoot trail. Pearl Hart kissed him good-bye and said she'd never forget him as she went on to lecture against sin. Sam Barca even insisted on buying him a drink after hours and agreed that if Kathy Doyle never spoke to Stringer again, he was likely ahead.

It wasn't so late when he finally got to his rooming house on Rincon Hill. But he sure wanted to lie down awhile.

As he slowly climbed the stairs in the gloom, he saw that, sure enough, the gal on the second landing had left her door ajar again. She was reclining on her big brass bedstead as usual, wearing no more than usual for a nude model. As she spotted him she blew tailormade cigarette smoke at him and called out, teasingly, "Where have you been all this time, Cowboy? You look as if a good meal and a bad woman would kill you."

He stared dully down at her curvacious naked body. "You're right," he said with a sigh. "Don't ever wind up between the sheets with anyone who just got out of prison. No offense, but you don't look nearly strong enough."